SPECIAL MESSAGE TO READERS

MOUNTAIN GOLD

Rex Brandon, internationally famous geologist, is flying to join a party of prospectors camped overlooking the frozen surface of Great Bear Lake in northern Canada, when his plane is forced down in a storm. Suddenly Brandon faces a 200-mile trek across the frozen wastes. Of the people he meets on his journey — all of whom want to get to Great Bear — several are destined to die, and Brandon cannot be certain that the survivors are who they say they are, or what their true motives may be . . .

DENIS HUGHES

◆

MOUNTAIN GOLD

Complete and Unabridged

LINFORD
Leicester

First published in Great Britain

First Linford Edition
published 2018

A catalogue record for this book is available
from the British Library.

ISBN 978–1–4448–3563–2

Published by
F. A. Thorpe (Publishing)
Anstey, Leicestershire

Set by Words & Graphics Ltd.
Anstey, Leicestershire
Printed and bound in Great Britain by
T.J. International Ltd., Padstow, Cornwall

This book is printed on acid-free paper

1

Blizzard!

Dawson, Keno City, Yukon, the Klondike . . . They were names with a past as well as a future; names to conjure with. In years gone by, men had struggled and died in the frozen wastes, seeking fabulous wealth, many finding only poverty and final death. And still men sought that wealth, drawn by the powerful magnet that lies in the name, the colour, the feel of gold.

But the new field of search was no longer in the boiling, tumultuous cities and towns that had sprung up more than half a century ago; nor was it centred in the barren mountains or dense pine forests of the Yukon. The new search, with new methods and new equipment to back it, moved approximately five hundred miles to the east.

Camped on the eastern slopes of the

Franklin Mountains, their pitch overlooking the frozen white surface of Great Bear Lake, were six people, five men and one woman. Not far from where they camped in a well-built log hut was the rising peak of Ectal-Borrn, its upper crags gleaming yellow where the savage wind had whipped away the snow cap. The natives had named Ectal-Borrn many hundreds of years before Europeans ever landed on the great American continent. They had named it from its colour, in their own local dialect. The Yellow Hill . . . The Golden Hill . . . Hill of Gold . . . Mountain Gold . . . And the party of tough, experienced prospectors on the slopes of the Franklin Mountains were there to prove that the mineral content of Ectal-Borrn was gold.

It was only recently that the party had arrived in this, their base camp. Spring was on the way. Before long the lake ice would break and pile, driven eastwards from the outfall of the thawing Mackenzie River; frozen snow would turn to mud, and the air would be warm and damp and alive with the buzz of mosquitoes. But not

2

yet. Here, only a few short miles from the Arctic Circle, the land was swept by wind, the last snows of winter were yet to fall, and the forests echoed eerily to the dismal howl of timber wolves, ranging in packs as they searched for food.

Not much in the way of actual prospecting had so far been done. For one thing, the party was not complete; and its leader, a man by the name of Hans Vetjek, preferred to wait till the last and seventh member of the party arrived. The days were as yet far too short to do much, and there was plenty of work for everyone before the yellow heart of Ectal-Borrn was examined and probed for its secret. The base camp must be made as snug as possible; supplies carefully cached against the greedy ravages of wolves and bears; every step planned in detail before the real work began when the snows disappeared and the long nights were divided by a few short hours of northern day, lengthening till there were no nights at all.

The last and seventh member of the party was already on his way. Rex

Brandon, a man to whom the lonely wastes of the earth were more home than cities, sat relaxed and easy in the cabin of a fast high-wing monoplane as it scudded east across the Ogilvie Range from Dawson, Yukon Territory.

There was one other passenger in the plane besides himself. Beyond a few words of greeting and an odd platitude here and there, little conversation took place. Brandon, after a brief study of his fellow passenger, had put him down as bag-man on his way to Norman Town. What he was selling mattered little. The man himself was small, insignificant, nervous and a fidget. He read a *Canadian Northwest Mountie* magazine for a while; but his eyes, pale and watery, were continually straying from the print to the grey-crested forests of pine and spruce below.

The pilot was a French-Canadian — lithe, dark and apt to be excitable in his speech and gestures. But he seemed to know his job well enough; and Brandon, accustomed as he was to almost every known form of travel, felt a flow of confidence in the man's ability.

As he sat there, he wondered what had urged him to answer Vetjek's invitation to join this affair. When he received it, he had been basking in the warmth and glow of the magic Mediterranean. The Yukon was a far cry from there, yet Brandon had accepted without hesitation, packing his gear and making all arrangements for a speedy trip to this land of cold and inhospitable snow and ice, forest and wolf-ridden terrain. It was Brandon's curse — or blessing — that he found it hard to refuse any offer that held promise of fresh fields to conquer; and it was some time since he had last used his wits against anything more terrible than the hazards of the African wilds. Vetjek's invitation, underlined by a genuine desire to assist his old friend and fellow geologist, had done the trick. But it was still something of a mystery to Brandon. He smiled as he stared out through the cabin window at the snow-clad peaks and glistening ice, the dark green masses of the forests and the misted hollows where the thaw was already setting in. The sky to the south was a pale, cold blue. Northward it changed to grey, finally ending in a piled-up wall of black and threatening nimbus clouds.

The pilot, Henri Frere, glanced apprehensively northward on several occasions. Brandon saw this, but made no comment. Nor did the other passenger. Henri was silent for a long time, watching the bank of cloud gradually wipe out all detail on the skyline. He had flown in these parts for years, and had come to treat with respect any sudden change in the weather. He was more than a little worried. There could be no turning back, for the climb over the Ogilvie Range, and through its narrow and treacherous passes to Dawson, was more than he was prepared to undertake with a blizzard in the offing. One mistake due to bad visibility would dash the plane against the pitiless rocks and glacial ice below. There was nothing for it but to carry on, hoping to make his destination before the oncoming blizzard struck.

'Snow coming up?' asked Brandon in a casual tone as he leant forward over the back of Henri's seat.

The pilot gave a nod and a shrug. '*M'sieu*, it is easy. We fly above the snow.'

Brandon frowned. 'You hope!' he said softly.

Henri shot him a warning glance. The other passenger was growing more restless the darker it became. 'We try, *m'sieu*. Do not worry.'

'*I* don't worry,' Brandon answered reassuringly. 'Get us through to Great Bear if you can.'

'But of course! *Mon dieu*, look at that!'

Brandon looked. The entire sky was blackening over. There was little doubt that the storm was breaking and would soon envelop them. Torn and broken clouds swept down from the north, forerunners of the opaque mass that followed them.

Henri cast an anxious glance ahead and south. The sky there was still clear, but thickening up rapidly in front of them. 'We run if we can, *m'sieu*!' he said, banking the plane to the south.

'Going to be a tough break,' said Brandon. He was beginning to appreciate the unpleasantness of their position. Though the plane winged south ahead of the blizzard, he was amazed to see that it still overhauled them fast.

The other passenger began mumbling to himself. His face had turned yellow with fear, and his hands fluttered to and fro in a peculiarly helpless fashion.

Henri set a fresh course on the compass. He tried to pinpoint his position on the ground, but the first mist of driven snow was already obscuring the scene. Snow and ice were beginning to build up on the wings of the aircraft. It seemed to labour as it flew, answering sluggishly to every move of the controls.

Then the full force of the blizzard struck them, blinding and frightening in its very opacity. A grey-white wall shut them in on every side, so that Henri cursed softly beneath his breath as he kept the plane steady by the instruments. Great fluky gales of wind came unexpectedly. The plane was hurled up in the sky, only to be pitched down at an angle again.

Brandon grabbed at the back of a

vacant seat to save himself being thrown from one side of the cabin to the other. He suddenly realised then that the other man, the nervous passenger, was lying still and silent, slumped in his seat.

Without calling Henri's attention, Brandon made a quick examination, securing the unconscious man's safety straps before doing his own. The man had been thrown violently against the side of the cabin by a lurch as the plane bumped savagely about the sky. His head was bruised on the temple. He would know little of what went on for the next few minutes at any rate, thought Brandon.

Henri was not in the least happy. He was trying to persuade the plane to climb above the blizzard, but even Brandon was able to tell from a glance at the instruments that he was having small success. Instead of climbing, the plane was slowly but surely being forced down closer to the now-invisible earth. The thought of what that earth consisted of was not a comfort to any man.

'Bad, eh?' said Brandon quietly. 'What

are the chances, Henri?'

The man gave a shrug. "Ow you say
... fifty-fifty,' he murmured gravely. 'I
'ave never known a storm to strike so
fast!'

Brandon's jaw hardened. 'We're not
done yet,' he said. 'Isn't there something
soft we can land on down there?' His
glance took in the altimeter. It was
reading only five hundred feet. Dawson,
whence they had come, lay at seven
hundred feet above sea level. The
altimeter was zeroed for that height.
They were therefore at roughly twelve
hundred feet above sea level, but the
foothills of the Ogilvie and Mackenzie
Mountains over which the plane was
flying were fifteen hundred feet. Brandon, with a sudden touch of uneasiness,
checked on Henri's map. He had no
more than a vague idea of their exact
position, but it was sufficient to make
him think about the earth. And the
further south they flew, the higher rose
the hills.

'Henri,' he said quietly, 'I make it that
we're only about a couple of hundred feet

or so above the ground.'

'*M'sieu*, it is the end, I think!'

Brandon stared out at the grey white wall of tumbling snow. Why had he come thousands of miles to perish in an aeroplane on some dreary barren slope? The spirit of adventure, he supposed. Was this to be the end?

Then, to his horrified gaze, a great naked spur of rock loomed up through the snow wrack, rushing towards them as the plane bucked and leapt in the turbulent currents of air. Henri gave a strangled yelp, whipping the stick over sharply. The spur of bare rock suddenly sheered away, then a down-draught took the plane in its grip and sent them rushing down at what seemed a terrifying angle. At the same time the propeller began to vibrate violently, its delicate balance upset by a lump of ice breaking loose from the leading edge of the wing and striking it near the tip.

Henri swore in his native tongue, switching off the engine.

Only the soughing of the wind past the fuselage and the dull roar of the storm beat against Brandon's eardrums.

And the plane, gliding now, being pitched and thrown as the whim of the blizzard dictated, rushed on through the grey world around it. Brandon's eyes were smarting from the strain of peering ahead, seeing nothing. What chance did they stand? He felt a fleeting pity for them all, then a strong sense of self-preservation gave him much-needed courage. He wasn't going to die! They'd never find his broken bones in the snow!

'Can we jump?' he said. His voice was tight and thin.

Henri opened his mouth to answer. Brandon was already fastening on his parachute, hurrying across to the unconscious bag-man and fixing his. Then Henri cried out sharply. A look through the Perspex of the cabin caused Brandon to grab at a seat back for support. For a second or two the whirling snow thinned and vanished, leaving the earth plain to see.

They were very low by this time, but to Brandon's joy it was not a landscape of jagged rocks and crags that swept up to meet them, but a shallow floored valley in the hills.

Henri gave a yell of triumph and hope. '*M'sieu*! *M'sieu*!' he shouted. 'We are saved!'

But the snow came down again, blinding and cutting them off from all sight of the ground. Brandon held his breath. If Henri made a single mistake now, it would all be over. The broad sweep of flat snow, at the end of which he had glimpsed a palisade of firs, was less than a hundred feet below.

Henri was suddenly incredibly calm and business-like. 'Your straps!' he said. 'It is best, yes!'

Brandon snapped them in position. Waiting. Waiting . . . Henri put the plane into a turn, winging round smoothly, the dead prop twirling slowly in front of him. Into wind . . . Blind. Henri slipped off a lot of height with a deftness that amazed Brandon. Then through the snow curtain he saw the ground, floating up at them swiftly. Henri checked the plane. Flaps at emergency. They came down like a lift, to be checked again at the last moment.

Even in the storm, Brandon could see the snow-covered ground, a great white blanket of space surrounded by and existing in a bubble of storm-torn air.

The plane, equipped with ski-landing gear, touched and bumped with a soggy feel. Snow was thrown up over the front of the cabin, curtaining off the view. Another bump, harder. Brandon felt himself forced against his straps. Suddenly there was a tearing, rending noise. The plane pitched forward, teetering on its nose, leaving them hanging in their seats. Henri was cursing. He had banged his head on the control panel. There was blood running down his forehead. Then everything was deathly still and silent. The interior of the cabin was almost pitch-dark. Nothing happened.

'We made it,' whispered Brandon. There was a vague note of surprise in his voice.

Henri turned his head and glared at him. There were tears starting from his liquid eyes. 'But the plane, she is broke!' he said. 'We hit a rock under the snow. 'Ow do I know it is there?'

Brandon was so relieved that he laughed. 'We're alive,' he said. 'That's all that matters at the moment. I didn't expect to get away with that, I can tell you!'

Henri grunted. 'As you say, *m'sieu*, we are alive, which is good. But — '

'But we have to get out of here and we're lost, is that it?' Brandon was still smiling, though the smile had a different quality now. He was seeing things from Henri's point of view. They were alive, but the prospects were far from being healthy: a blizzard in the foothills, with maybe a hundred-mile trek ahead of them through unknown country, and neither food nor proper equipment to face it. No, he thought grimly, it was not a pleasant prospect.

The cold began to creep in through the cabin sides. An icy draught whistled down Brandon's neck as he sat there deep in thought. 'We shall have to stay put till the snow stops,' he said.

Henri grinned for the first time. '*M'sieu* is right,' he agreed. 'You like hot coffee, yes?' He reached into a nail locker underneath his seat, producing a large thermos ask.

'Thank you,' murmured Brandon gratefully. He put on a heavy fur-lined top-coat. It was getting colder now that any heat from the engine had been cut off.

Henri poured a cup and passed it over with a smile and a nod. Brandon, cheerful again, accepted it and stood up on the steeply slanting floor of the cabin. The plane had come to a stop with its engine partly buried in the snow, tail cocked up at nearly twenty degrees from the horizontal. The drift of snow, and a submerged rock, had wrought a consider-able amount of damage, but until they could examine it properly it was not possible to tell if Henri would be able to get the plane off the ground again. Brandon kept his fingers crossed, and together the two of them went to work on the heavily breathing bag-man. He came round after a minute or two, peering about in a dazed way.

'Jeez!' he muttered suddenly. 'I can still breathe! Ain't that funny?' He blinked his watery eyes at Brandon.

'Funny peculiar, or funny ha-ha?' said Brandon, grinning. 'Here, have some coffee. We made a forced landing, if it's of any interest to you.'

The man grunted dismally. 'Ain't that wonderful?' he said. 'Me, I'm turning this job right in the moment I see my boss. He can hawk his stuff himself!'

'Salesman?' queried Brandon sympathetically.

The little man nodded. 'Sure,' he said, sipping his coffee and feeling the bump on his temple.

'What do you sell? Any samples we'd find useful at the moment?' Brandon glanced at the three heavy suitcases that comprised the man's luggage.

The little man laughed, a tinny sound. 'If we had a bathroom and a toilet, I could set us up for life with a dozen things to keep the drains sweet. Laugh that off, brother!'

Oddly enough, Brandon did so, as did Henri Frere. The little man eyed them with a sceptical grin. Then he, too, was laughing.

'I am never so 'appy!' said Henri. 'Are we not alive, my friends? Come! More coffee! Your good health, yes!'

2

Full House

The cold became more and more penetrating. Muffled up in all the spare clothing they had, the three men waited as patiently as they could for the blizzard to abate. Snow was drifting thickly over the aircraft, and before long the inside of the cabin was so dark that Henri switched on the lights. The sound of the wind gradually dropped, but Brandon could not be sure whether this was due to the fact that the plane was being buried, or whether the storm was blowing itself out. By the end of an hour after their landing he was growing restless, and a short time later announced his intention of leaving the cabin and taking a look outside.

'Imbecile!' said Henri. 'You get lost, m'sieu!'

Brandon said no, he wouldn't get lost. There was no sense in staying where they were once the storm abated. It might be a considerable time before any searching aircraft saw them, and the obvious thing to do was find shelter of some kind and keep a big fire going until it was sighted. The plane itself might never be seen from the air, but a fire certainly would be. In the end the others were forced to agree, but it was left to Brandon to make the initial sortie into the cold and cheerless world outside.

Getting out of the aircraft was simpler than he had expected. Henri lent a hand in forcing the door back on the weight of snow that was drifted against it, and then Brandon was overjoyed to see that the sky was visible and the storm had died down. He scrambled out, floundering in waist-deep snow. The wind, still fairly strong, sent a flurry of drift against his face, but the falling snow had ceased and the sky was a cold, hard steely colour. But away to the north showed a hint of very dark blue, a thin promise of better weather.

'Come on out!' he called to the others. 'There are trees about half a mile west. We're in a valley.'

Reluctantly the little bag-man followed him out, nearly disappearing in a drift. Henri came last, plainly unhappy about leaving his plane. To Henri the stranded craft still represented home. He was not used to this world of snow and lifeless, wind-swept country. But the force of leadership in Brandon gave him fresh determination. He followed like a lamb as the tall broad-shouldered Englishman started off in the direction of the tree-line nearest the plane. The side of the valley rose more steeply, giving shelter from the wind. Soon there was only a faint murmur as it sighed over the uneven surface of the snow, piling it in little ridges, drifting it deep against outcrops such as the one that had brought the plane to grief on landing. They were lucky to have got away with it so lightly, thought Brandon. They were lucky to have got away with it at all.

Progress towards the tall snow-capped pines and spruce was slow. The bag-man blundered along unhappily, muttering a great deal of invective as he went. Henri and Brandon, tougher beings, were glad enough when they crossed the last ridge and paused for breath in the cold, gloomy shelter of the forest.

'*M'sieu*, what now?' queried Henri plaintively. 'We are 'ere in the trees, but that is all. I do not like it.'

'You two stay here while I do a recce,' said Brandon.

Henri spread his hands. '*Mon Dieu!*' he groaned. 'You will 'urry, yes? The cold, she is bad!'

Brandon, guided more by the instinct of a hunter than by anything else, set off through the trees. Less than half a mile from where he had left the others, he came upon something that raised his spirits enormously. There in the snow was a baited trap. Calling on all his knowledge of the wilds, he moved on, to find another not far away. This was trapper country. He had not been wrong in his guess. And a trap line meant the human element. He plunged on, again guided by instinct and knowledge.

When he found what he sought, it was very much nearer than he had dared to hope. Fifty yards ahead, in a small cleared space in the forest, stood a low, solid-looking log cabin, its angled roof thick with snow. There was a deserted atmosphere about it as he approached. The door was shut, and no sign of smoke issued from the squat chimney-piece that showed at the rear. In front of the building the snow lay undisturbed except for a line of wolf tracks that circled the place at a distance.

'No one at home,' murmured Brandon. He was growing accustomed to the biting cold by now, but approached with instinctive caution, making a complete circuit of the cabin before finally going to the door.

A crude hasp fastened it on the outside. He opened the door and peered in. A stale smell greeted him; but the sight of familiar objects, and most of all a pot-bellied stove in the middle of the floor, brought a satisfied smile to his face. Whoever the owner was, he would not be likely to object to their making use of his home.

Without entering, he turned away, closing the door behind him, and struck

off to fetch his two companions. At the
news that he had found a dwelling,
Henri's spirits rose like a barometer in an
anticyclone, and even the little bag-man
cheered up enormously. 'Maybe the guy
who lives there has a bathroom and
toilet!' he said hopefully. 'Think of the
commission, brother!'

Brandon grinned as the three of them
walked into the clearing. Henri gave a
whoop of pleasure at sight of the cabin.
He capered about in the snow, falling into
a drift in his excitement and relief. By the
time they had extricated him, he was
feeling in a more sober frame of mind.

Once they were inside the cabin, it was
not long before the hazards and discom-
fort of the past few hours were forgotten.
A fire was lit in the stove; warmth seeped
through the cabin, finding every nook and
cranny and staying there. Brandon, old
hand as he was at fending for himself
under trying circumstances, quickly discovered a mass of tinned food, and in no
time at all they were sitting round the
rude pine table drinking scalding soup
and wolfing some of the finest canned

steak they had ever tasted.

There was only one bunk, but plenty of blankets for all; and when the meal was finished and cleared away, the other two turned in on Brandon's suggestion, leaving him seated at the table with a large-scale map he had brought from the plane.

Outside, the short day was ended. Night clamped down with an icy hand, and the stillness of the surrounding forest was only broken by a distant and incredibly mournful wolf cry. Then the little bag-man started snoring where he lay on the floor, cocooned in blankets in front of the stove, the top of which glowed cherry-red.

Brandon sighed, folded the map and thrust it in his inner pocket. He thought he knew where they were, and as far as he could see there was nothing to choose between making for Great Bear Lake or striking back towards Dawson. Dawson was considerably closer, but it would entail a crossing of the Ogilvie Range. If they bypassed the mountains, the distance was even greater than to Great

Bear. A lot would depend on what attitude Henri adopted. After all, thought Brandon, the pilot might think it better to remain in the cabin and wait for rescue. The same went for the bag-man.

Brandon realised he had never discovered what the little man's name was. Not that it mattered a lot. In any case, he was not built for breaking a trail in this sort of country. But with Brandon himself it was a different story. He wanted to be at Great Bear Lake, and unless he set out to reach it he might never get there till summer. In the end he decided to wait until he could discuss the position with his companions. It would hardly be fair to leave them on their own unless they were willing. Everything was quiet, save for the soft whisper of the wind among the tree-tops. Brandon yawned, stretched his arms, and glanced at the sleeping forms of his two oddly assorted companions. Then he wrapped himself in a blanket and went to sleep on the other side of the stove.

The snarling and yapping of a dog team aroused him. He sat up with a jerk and rubbed the sleep from his eyes. A gruff voice was cursing the dogs outside. Brandon scrambled from his blanket and made for the door, but before he could get it open it was thrown back on its rawhide hinges and a fur-muffled figure stood on the threshold, cold air sweeping in past him. Henri and the bag-man slumbered on undisturbed. Brandon and the newcomer looked at each other, sizing up, not yet sure what attitude to take. The man in the furs was a giant. He gripped a rifle in one mitted fist, keeping it pointing in the general direction of Brandon. His face was barely visible, what with the fur-lined hood of his clothing and the heavy black beard that concealed his jaw. His nose was a great sharp hook, almost meeting the hair of his moustache. Brandon concentrated on his eyes. They were large, dark and widely spaced. Outside, the dogs were snarling restlessly.

'Made yourself at home, I see,' said the man with a grin. His teeth, when they showed briefly, were white and even. He was younger than Brandon had thought at first.

'Sorry to be so free in here,' said Brandon. 'We were lucky to find this cabin, I reckon. Plane came down about a mile from here.' He kept his voice low, glancing meaningfully at the rifle that still covered him in a casual fashion.

The other man grunted. 'Darned things, them aeroplanes,' he commented dryly. 'Come and give me a hand with the dogs, friend. They're sort of frisky. Plenty of wolves around.'

Brandon knew he had been accepted. This man, lonely and inclined to be taciturn, was not the demonstrative type. A friendly word was all he would say; after that it was up to Brandon and his companions.

As if to confirm acceptance, the man leant his rifle against the door frame and turned away. Brandon followed him out through the door, where the dog team, still harnessed to a sled, was tangling itself up in a bickering free-for-all of snapping jaws and bared fangs. Without being bitten, which to Brandon seemed a miracle, they loosed the dogs and stowed the sled gear. Then the man fetched several great chunks of raw meat from a lean-to at the back of the cabin. When he tossed them to the dogs it might have been a wolf pack in full cry, the din was so great.

'Ought to wake your buddies, friend,' said the man. 'Come on inside again. I could do with something hot.'

Brandon glanced at the pile of pelts on the sled. His host was a trapper, undoubtedly. He reflected on the lonely life it must be, but said nothing. They moved towards the cabin again. The dogs, ten of the biggest huskies Brandon had ever seen, were eating contentedly. Presently they would curl up in the snow and sleep.

Henri was sitting up in the bunk when they entered. He shot a somewhat nervous glance at Brandon when he caught sight of the trapper. The man gave a curt nod. As soon as the door was shut, he peeled off his heavy top clothing and blew some warmth into his cupped hands. Brandon stirred the stove and woke the little bag-man, who blinked.

Brandon introduced Henri, gesturing

to the bag-man as well. 'This is our host,' he added. 'We're lucky to have found such a comfortable spot in trouble.'

Henri gave a little bow of his head, smiling as he did so. 'Bravo!' he murmured fervently. 'I am so 'appy to be 'ere, I can tell you.'

The trapper eyed him shrewdly for a moment. 'Forget it, friend,' he said slowly. 'In these parts there aren't any boundaries. Not like the rest of the world . . . You're welcome to stick around as long as you like. Is your plane badly damaged?'

Henri shrugged. 'I cannot tell till we examine it,' he replied. 'Maybe not; then I take off again.'

The trapper stirred soup on the stove top mechanically. 'There's more snow coming,' he said. His voice was deep and slow, as if he was not accustomed to talking to people. 'If you're wise, you'll remain here. Plenty food and warmth. Be fools to leave.'

'We're much obliged to you,' put in Brandon. 'But — '

The man grinned suddenly. 'Forget the

30

'buts',' he said. 'It's nine months since I talked to a white man. In another four weeks I'll be moving my stuff out to Norman, a whole winter's crop of pelts. That's quite a lot. You can make the trip with me if you're minded. The name's Jake, by the way. Jake Dempster, one time of London.' He turned to Brandon. 'You're a Limey, aren't you?'

Brandon nodded. 'That's right,' he said. 'Didn't expect to meet another out here.'

Jake gave a shrug. 'Been my home for twenty-five years now,' he said. 'I guess a man gets attached to a certain way of life and it goes against the grain to make a break.' He smiled in a faraway fashion. 'One time I wanted a pub in the Old Kent Road. That was when I was a kid.' He eyed Brandon. 'Now you, you wouldn't be happy stuck away from people for three-quarters of the year. Only the trees and the snow and the wolves for company ... Gets sort of lonesome at times, but I wouldn't change now for the world.'

Brandon smiled understandingly. He

said nothing of his own penchant for living beyond the pale of civilisation, but he understood. There was a strong affinity between himself and Jake. He felt they could grow to be good friends if they had the opportunity.

The little bag-man grunted in a disconsolate manner. He was far from happy in his own mind. The burly trapper actually scared him. He could not understand a man like this. Once again, he wondered and asked himself why in the world he had taken on the thankless job of trying to sell things in these frozen, unfriendly wastes. There was no answer to the question. There never would be. The little man gave it up and decided to get some more sleep. His eyelids were incredibly heavy even now. Sanitary disinfectants! These primitive men of the wilds had never heard of such modern facilities! The little man was weary.

But no sooner had he gone to sleep before there was more disturbance. Brandon and Jake were talking quietly. Brandon had the map spread out on the cabin table, checking their position with the trapper. Henri was cleaning his fingernails, listening to the other two, thinking about his aircraft and weighing the chances of a take-off. He was reasonably content to let things take their course at the moment. And anyway, the plane was insured. Still, it was bad for business.

Suddenly Jake sat up straight, head to one side, an intense expression on his bearded face. What his sharp ears had detected even Brandon could not guess. Jake held up a hand, listening. There was a faint frown on his brow.

A moment later Brandon, too, heard the distant yapping of dogs. It was taken up and echoed and drowned by the clamour of Jake's own team, roused from their slumber. Henri put his nail file away and stood up questioningly.

'More visitors!' grunted Jake tersely. 'Busy tonight, friends!'

'They're coming this way?' said Brandon.

Jake merely nodded, rising to his feet and striding to the door. As he threw it open, a blast of icy air came in. The blankets over the bag-man lifted in the draught. He gave a muttered curse and huddled closer to the roaring stove. But Jake only stood in the open doorway, with Brandon and Henri at his back.

The cry of the dogs was coming closer. Somewhere in the distance behind it, the howling of wolves was plainly audible.

Jake turned and picked up his rifle. 'Bring the lamp, friend,' he said curtly. 'May be lost.'

Brandon fetched the oil lamp from the table. The sound of the team was rapidly increasing. They could hear it even above the din of Jake's huskies.

Then they saw them: a line of leaping black dots on the cold white surface of the snow at the far end of the clearing. It was dark, but with a luminous quality in the darkness. The dots grew larger, more distinct. They leapt and strained in front of a sled. A figure ran silently over the snow in the rear, grasping the sled handles firmly.

'Injun,' grunted Jake.

'How do you know?'

'By the way he moves on snow.'

Brandon was waving the lamp to and fro. It must have been a welcome sight to the team and the man who drove it.

They heard his voice urging the dogs on to greater speed. The team swung in towards the light of Brandon's lamp. None of the men in the doorway stirred. They only waited. Then the team came to a panting stop, snapping and snarling at the dogs of Jake's line as they sniffed and growled vindictively at the newcomers.

The dark figure walked smoothly towards them, moving with effortless ease on the snowshoes he wore. He was a northern Indian, and his right hand was raised in a sign of peace as he blinked in the light of the lamp.

'Come on in,' said Jake. 'Get caught in the blizzard?'

The Indian merely nodded, then gestured to the snow-covered sled. 'White woman,' he said. 'Pay well, but fool.'

Brandon stared past him at the sled. What he had thought to be a pile of gear was stirring to life. It rose stiffly as he went towards it, detaching itself from the furs on top of the sled. It was a person all right, and as the figure walked towards him he saw it was indeed a woman.

'Come on in,' he said tritely, echoing Jake's words of welcome. He did not know what nationality she might be, but her answer put him at ease.

'What a country!' she said. 'You're the first human beings I've met since leaving Dawson. That Indian just isn't human, believe me!'

3

'Get Your Gun, Friend'

The Indian passed in through the door of the cabin. Jake waited for Brandon and the woman, while Henri hovered in the background. The little bag-man was snoring again.

With a strangely dignified bearing in one so large and roughly clad, Jake greeted the woman and ushered her in with a faint smile. She thanked him gratefully, but to Brandon's eye it was plain that she had had enough and must be close to exhaustion. He wondered what on earth a young woman like her was doing out in the wilds in such uncertain weather, and remembered her mention of having left Dawson. Had she really come all this way with the Indian?

In a few minutes they were all gathered round the table again. Hot coffee and soup were in plentiful supply, and under its warming influence the woman, who when she took off her outer garments was revealed as being slim and unexpectedly attractive, began to relax in a state of obvious relief. Yet there was an odd reserve about her answers when Brandon tried to find out what she was doing and where she was bound for. He had a feeling that she was hedging all the time, and was, moreover, using the excuse of her tiredness to put off direct replies as to her destination. Out of consideration for her he did not press his enquiries, but exchanged a glance with Jake that was full of meaning and unspoken questions.

Jake shrugged, unnoticed by the woman; then a moment later Henri offered her the comfort of the bunk he had vacated, and she accepted it readily enough.

Jake, meanwhile, after a glance at an ancient turnip watch that he dragged ponderously from his inner pocket, went across to a cupboard in the corner of the room and rummaged about inside. Brandon watched him curiously, suppressing a whistle of surprise when the trapper produced a small wireless receiver and placed it carefully on the table. It was obvious from the way he handled it that the radio was a precious thing, and his smile when he met Brandon's eyes was one of pride.

'Only thing I hide when I go on the trap-line,' he said. 'Batteries difficult to get in these parts, friend. Can't waste 'em!'

'You're pretty fortunate to have a radio at all, I should think,' said Brandon.

Jake was fiddling with the controls, his great bulk bent over the table. 'I traded a couple of cans of beans for it with an Injun,' he volunteered. 'The batteries had run out and the poor guy didn't think it was any good!' He gave a deep-throated chuckle. Then the radio crackled and the nasal voice of an announcer filled the cabin. 'Usually listen to newscasts when I'm home.'

The announcer was talking fast about baseball. A big game had recently been won by a world-famous team at Yankee Stadium. Jake seemed to be intensely interested; Brandon did not understand baseball. Henri grew quite excited, and the little man slept on undisturbed by such world-shaking events.

The woman in the bunk lay with her hands folded behind her head. The lamplight gleamed in her short curly hair. It was crisp and warm like a maize field just before harvest. Her nose was short and slightly tilted as she stared up at the chinks in the roof, watching a spider scuttle into view as if on an urgent mission.

The announcer said: 'And now folks, here are a few other items of news.' He was a little out of breath. 'From the U.S. research base in northern Alaska, word has leaked that Nicolas Shawn, foremost atomic expert and scientist of high reputation, has disappeared. This man is in possession of, and for several years past has had access to, most of the major secrets of U.S. advancement in the field of atomic research. No official announcement has been made, but it is thought that Shawn headed east after disappearing. This agency is not alarmist, folks, but we feel it our duty to impress on the public the potential danger represented by men such as this who may possibly be willing to barter their nationalist duty for a handful of doubtful currency.'

Jake raised his eyebrows, shrugging his massive shoulders.

The woman in the bunk stirred restlessly. 'Turn it off,' she said. 'Please . . . ' Her voice was ragged at the edges.

Jake glanced across at her enquiringly.

Henri blinked and started to speak, then changed his mind. The woman was pale and her mouth was set.

Jake smiled reassuringly. "Fraid we disturbed you, miss,' he said. 'Sorry.' He leant forward and turned off the radio.

She pulled herself together with an obvious effort. Her tongue touched her lips and she seemed to relax.

'My — my head aches,' she mumbled. 'Forgive me, all of you.'

Jake went on watching her, silent now. Brandon cleared his throat loudly. Headache? There *was* something on her mind, without doubt, but not that kind of ache.

'Poor leetle one,' murmured Henri

consolingly. 'We be silent, yes? You sleep, *m'anisette.*' He nodded and smiled.

Brandon said nothing, but his eyes still rested on the woman. He was beginning to wonder a lot of things about her. Who was she? Where did she come from? Where was she going? They were queries he could not answer, and something, some inner instinct, warned him not to question her openly. Under cover of the headache she professed, she lay down again, this time with her face towards the wall of the cabin.

Brandon and Jake exchanged looks. Henri wore a puzzled frown. The little man on the floor slept on. Elko, the Indian who had brought the woman, sighed and rubbed his chin, turning over in his blankets and going to sleep without a word.

No one spoke. Presently Jake gave a shrug and turned down the lamp. 'What say we turn in, friend?' he said quietly.

Brandon nodded. All manner of different thoughts were ploughing about in his mind, most of them centred on the woman with the red-gold hair and the tilted nose. However deceptive first impressions might be, he felt sure she was on the level; yet there was something wrong somewhere. He curled himself up on the floor and tried to sleep. A man who could usually sleep or wake under any circumstances, even Brandon found it difficult on this occasion.

It was the noise of the trapper moving around that wakened him. He looked up and blinked in the lamplight, then sat up, yawning and stretching.

'Breakfast, friend,' grunted Jake. 'Caribou steak!'

'Sounds good to me,' answered Brandon. He got up and looked round the cabin. The air was clammy, hot and none too fresh. Outside, the dogs were stirring, making their own kind of clamour, the two teams mixing cautiously.

Elko stirred and went outside, letting in the cold, dark air of an indeterminate dawn. A flurry of snowflakes wisped in through the door as he opened it. Against the mutter of the wind in the pines, Brandon thought he heard the soft, muted patter of falling snow.

'More of it,' said Jake, reading his thoughts. 'Plenty more, friend. Maybe a week before anyone moves out of here.'

Brandon shot a glance at the hump in the trapper's bunk. The woman was breathing slowly and deeply. There was a healthy rhythm about it. But he went on wondering, watching her as Jake boiled water and brewed up coffee. The splutter of a frying pan on the top of the stove woke Henri. Elko came back inside the cabin. His face was completely unreadable. When he moved, he made so little noise that he might have been a ghost, albeit a very solid one. Henri ruffled his hair, grinned at Brandon and glanced at the occupied bunk. Then he prodded the little bag-man into wakefulness. He sat up, rubbed his eyes and ran his tongue round the inside of his mouth. It must have tasted terrible from the look on his nondescript face. He shuddered violently and scrambled to his feet.

'Breakfast,' said Jake more loudly. 'Day only lasts a few hours this time o' year. Better take a look at that plane of yours while it's light.'

Henri remembered the aircraft and tried not to look worried. He was really enjoying himself quite a lot. Pity to spoil it, he thought. But Jake was right.

The woman took an interest in life a few moments later. When she sat up, there was none of the strain in her eyes that Brandon had glimpsed the previous evening. In fact he was pleasantly surprised when she wished everyone good morning and started talking more freely than before. He led her on as they all sat down to a meal at the rough pine table in the centre of the cabin floor. But although he led the conversation round several times to what her plans were, he found himself baulked at every turn. She was very sweet and polite, but a whole lot more evasive than he had thought anyone could possibly be. And the fact that she managed it without giving any offence only made matters worse.

When the meal was over, she looked round expectantly. 'Did I hear you say you were going to look at a plane?' she asked quietly. 'I suppose there's no chance of making a takeoff, is there? I particularly want to finish my journey, you see, and I wondered . . . '

But Henri only shrugged and shook his head. '*M'amselle*,' he answered disconsolately, 'we 'ave crashed. We are stuck 'ere, as you would say. It is bad. You wait maybe a week, an' we take you with us.'

Her face fell in disappointment. 'Never mind,' she said. 'Will you think me very rude if I ask for a little privacy while I wash and have a clean-up in here? I feel filthy.'

'Of course,' said Brandon. 'Henri, what about taking a look at the kite?'

'Immediately, *m'sieu*.' It is what I intended.'

'I'll go along with you, friend,' rumbled Jake. 'What about the Injun, miss?'

She hesitated. 'He can see to the dogs,' she said. 'I don't think there's any need to worry about Elko.'

'There's a rifle yonder,' said Jake.

She nodded and smiled. 'Thank you,' she murmured. 'And — thank you for everything.' In a suddenly impetuous fashion, she thrust out her hand towards him, watching his face with her sombre

46

light brown eyes, smiling warmly all the time.

Jake grunted uncomfortably. 'Forget it, ma'am,' he replied. 'You're welcome here.' But he took her hand in his great fingers and held it for an instant.

She watched them go from the doorway, a small, slight figure without her furs. There was a fine drift of snow round her feet as she lifted a hand and waved when Brandon looked back. Round at the side of the cabin, he saw Elko kneeling down in the snow, mending a broken trace and surrounded by dogs, to which he spoke strange-sounding words.

The little bag-man did not enjoy his trip to the plane. It was only the strength of Jake's arm that kept him upright most of the time. When they finally reached the aircraft, his spirits dropped even lower when Henri, after a brief but thorough examination, announced in a gloomy voice that it would take at least a week to put the machine in serviceable condition again.

Brandon took the opportunity of retrieving his big-game rifle from his luggage; and when they started off again for the cabin, they were all loaded down with extra clothes and other items of baggage, Jake carrying all the little man's gear as if its weight was nothing.

They were out of the valley where the plane had landed, and deep in the tree belt that screened them from the cabin clearing, when the trapper halted abruptly, head to one side, listening. Brandon and Henri stopped. The bag-man sank to his waist in a drift and stayed there miserably. In the distance they could hear the yapping of dogs, and a moment later Jake uttered a muttered curse as the sounds of Elko's 'Mush! Mush!' reached his ears.

'It's that blamed fool woman!' he said savagely. 'What does she think she's up to?'

'Slipping off,' said Brandon. 'Come on, man, hurry! We've got to stop her.' He glanced up at the sky, where it showed dark and ominous between the trees. There was more snow coming, the first flakes already sprinkling down through the foliage. A queer sort of hush fell on the forest. The moan of wind was muffled, then gradually rose as Brandon and Jake plunged on ahead, leaving Henri to bring up the rear with his companion.

With a sinking heart, Brandon realised that the yapping of the dog team was gradually fading. They were too late. Floundering into the clearing, they saw the cabin empty and deserted. Clearly defined sled marks ran away at an angle and disappeared among the trees, following a game trail.

'I suppose she *has* gone,' grunted Brandon. 'Not just Elko, I mean.' He ran for the cabin door, glancing inside. But the woman was no longer there. There was a note on the table, hurriedly written. Pinned to it was some paper money. Brandon scanned the note. 'Many thanks,' he read. 'Please don't think me ungrateful, and try to forgive me for acting like this. The money is for the rifle I've taken.' He glanced up as Jake came thumping in. 'She's borrowed your rifle. Can we catch her up, Jake? She'll never make it with another storm brewing. Idiot!'

Jake grinned, despite his inner feelings. 'I'll get the dogs harnessed up,' he said curtly. 'Never mind the rifle; I've got another.' He disappeared outside again, calling his team together.

They were almost ready to leave when Henri and the bag-man arrived, out of breath and labouring in the snow. Jake was hurriedly packing food and various odds and ends on the sled. '*M'sieu*, where you go?' demanded Henri breathlessly.

'Depends on the lady!' answered Brandon. 'She's leading us a dance, by the look of it.'

Henri hissed under his breath. 'We go with you,' he said.

'Impossible,' answered Jake. 'You two stick around. Make this your home for as long as you like; and don't forget there's another blizzard on the way, if I'm anything of a judge.'

'Be seeing you,' said Brandon, piling onto the sled as the trapper gripped the hand rails at the rear and yelled at the team. His long whip licked out and cracked in the air. The dogs strained forward in their traces, barking joyously.

Brandon looked at the bag-man alongside. 'What's your name?' he asked suddenly.

The sled began to move forward. The bag-man grinned almost cheerfully. 'Archibald,' he said. 'Archibald Ramshorn. Good, isn't it?'

The team swung away, getting into their stride. Archie's last words were whipped up in flying snow and drowned.

'Mush! Mush!' shouted Jake. Then he yelled at the dogs individually, naming them. Victor . . . Baron . . . Silver . . . Don . . . They seemed to take on fresh cloaks of canine energy, and before long the sled was skimming crisply over the snow as it followed the trail of the woman and the Indian.

'Heading east by north,' observed Brandon.

'Maybe trying to cross the Mackenzie,' answered Jake. 'They'll be lucky if they make it. The country 'tween here and there is alive with wolves. Maybe the Injun knows what he's doing, and I reckon she paid him well, but she's still a darned fool!'

Brandon silently agreed. The sled whooshed onwards, for the trail was easy to follow and the going good. At first they climbed through standing pine and spruce. It was a silent grey-white world of twilight, with nothing moving save the leaping dogs out in front of the sled. The only sound audible was the singing of the steel sled runners and occasional cries from Jake as he urged his team on. He seemed completely tireless, loping along in the rear of the sled with an easy stride.

Then the trail began to drop away through the trees. It was swinging on a more easterly course, picking the simplest route through the forest.

'That Injun's no mean hand,' commented Jake. 'I guess he knows this country near as well as I do.'

'Let's hope you're right,' said Brandon. 'Look, there's a clearing ahead. They went straight across it.'

'Good enough!' said Jake. Without warning, he swung the team off at a tangent, sending the dogs in through the trees at a fast run.

'What's the matter?' demanded Brandon.

'Going that way, they must turn sharp right in less than a half mile, friend,' answered the trapper. 'There's a ravine, and it leaves only one way to go. We can cut off a whole chunk of country and shorten their lead. Seems that Injun ain't so bright after all!' He laughed, baring his teeth in the bitter wind of their progress.

More snow was falling now, crusting on their furs. The breath of the panting dogs rose in clouds, mingling with the spindrift as it gouted up from their paws. Jake's breath was frosting on his beard, hoaring it over till the whole adornment was stiff and white. Brandon checked his rifle magazine, loading the gun and putting the safety catch to safe.

They sped on in silence, neither man speaking. The ground was still falling away, so that Jake had to check the speed of the dogs a little, riding on the back end of the runners. 'Break in the trees coming soon,' he shouted to Brandon. 'We stop then and see where they are. Maybe they haven't got past, then we cut 'em off!'

The trees thinned abruptly, giving way to a great sweep of virgin snow, gleaming ghostly in the pale daylight. Jake brought the team to a flank-heaving stop. The dogs flopped down in the snow of their own accord. From where they were in the fringe of the tree-line, the men commanded a view of the entire open space to the north and east. Nothing moved on the bare blanket of the snow. Nor were there any sled tracks visible.

'We're in luck,' observed Jake in a satisfied tone. 'They haven't passed. All we have to do is — ' He stopped abruptly, biting the sentence off unfinished. The dogs were creating a lot of noise, but he silenced them with a gesture.

From what seemed a great distance, there came the clamour of another team. But it was not that which made Brandon stiffen and strain his ears. The dismal howling of a wolf pack was mingled and mixed with the baying of the dogs.

Jake drew a deep breath. The noise was coming steadily closer. 'Get your gun, friend,' he said grimly. His own dogs were growing restive again, listening, whining among themselves. He silenced them with a curt but effective word. The team leader, Baron, an enormous grey-brown beast with the shoulders of a young bull, eyed his master with plain respect. He was an almost human animal.

Brandon took his gun from the sled, handing Jake his as well. They waited, tense and silent. Suddenly the distance was split by the crack of a rifle. The howling of the wolf pack increased in its clamour.

And then, as far to the east as they could see, there was movement. Grey loping shapes came into view. They were out in front and on all sides of the small strung-out line of a dog team. A squat figure plodded anxiously along in the rear of the sled. From the sled itself a gun rapped out once more. One of the grey shapes somersaulted, to be fallen on by its savage comrades. It looked like a running fight.

4

How Far to Great Bear?

'Hold your fire,' muttered Jake. 'Wait till we can be sure of a hit.' He glanced at Brandon sideways. 'Have you done much shooting, friend?'

Brandon concealed a faint smile. 'Just a little,' he admitted.

They went on waiting in strained silence. Brandon was estimating the range with narrowed eyes. Seven hundred yards . . . Any minute now. Jake brought his rifle up to the shoulder, sighting carefully. The icy cold bit their fingers. Brandon cuddled the stock of his own gun. Six hundred yards.

'Right!' he breathed. 'Let 'em have it!'

The two guns cracked almost simultaneously, their echoes reverberating among the trees at their backs. Two of the grey-coated wolves went flying in the snow. But more of the beasts were closing in on the little team. Even as Jake re-cocked his rifle, one of the grey shapes leapt full-tilt at the figure of Elko, the Indian. The rifle cracked from the sled itself as the woman fired in desperation. Brandon's gun hammered out, but before his bullet killed the wolf poor Elko was down in the snow. The body of the wolf fell across him. In an instant the team had dragged the sled onwards. The gap between the Indian and the woman widened rapidly as the panic-stricken dogs raced on. Before the eyes of Brandon and Jake, Elko disappeared in a fighting tangle of savage jaws and lean grey bodies. Meanwhile, the woman on the sled was firing as quickly as she could, for the remainder of the wolf pack were pressing the team even more closely. The wolves grew bolder, but the range was decreasing rapidly. By this time, Brandon and Jake were pumping out shots as fast as they could load and aim. More than a dozen of the wolves had been killed, and the woman herself had accounted for four. But still the wolves kept pressing in on every side, till it looked as if the sled itself would be overwhelmed.

'Come on!' yelled Brandon fiercely. 'Charge 'em or they'll get her!'

Jake gave a grunt of approval, firing one more shot before moving. Then he and Brandon were running down the slope overlooking the scene of the desperate battle. Brandon fired as he ran, commando fashion, from the hip. They had less than fifty yards to go now. The woman saw them, dragging the team around so that it tore towards them. Then three of the boldest creatures hurled themselves at the leading dogs, dragging them down. In a moment the team was fighting and snarling, tangled in its harness, striving to tear themselves loose and defend themselves against the savage attack of the timber beasts. The woman saw her danger. When Brandon and the trapper were still several yards away, she jumped from the sled and raced to meet them. Brandon dropped the animal closest to her. Jake went on firing, cool and accurate. The woman's face was pale and drawn. She stumbled so that another of the ravening wolves made a leap that almost carried it on top of her. Only a timely bullet from Brandon's rifle stopped it in the nick of time. Then Jake grabbed her arm as she floundered up to them.

'Get her back to the trees!' snapped Brandon curtly. He went on shooting, snapping a fresh magazine into his gun.

Jake wasted no time on words. The woman made a faint protest, but his grip was strong, and the two of them started back for the tree-line, leaving Brandon to stem the oncoming pack, which was now somewhat broken and scattered but still vindictive at losing its prey.

Standing there, a solitary figure against the white ground of the open space, Brandon called on all his skill and speed of action. The grey shapes flung themselves towards him, but his trigger finger worked with as much smooth precision as ever. The vanguard hesitated, breaking in the face of his deadly fire. Another magazine was emptied, to be replaced by a fresh one. Then Jake was shouting to him from the tree-line close by the restless team of dogs. Brandon glanced over his shoulder as the trapper started shooting again, giving him covering fire. Brandon seized the chance and turned his back on the wolves, running through the foot-deep snow as bullets whistled past him from Jake's rifle. He saw that the woman was sitting on the sled, head in hands, exhausted from her ordeal. Behind him, the wolves were yelping and snarling as they fought over the remnants of the beaten dog team and the body of Elko. The noise gradually lessened. By the time he reached the trapper's side, the pack had dispersed.

'Quite a fight while it lasted,' commented Jake. He eyed Brandon with new respect as the famous geologist and big-game hunter came to a halt. 'You're not as new to this sort of thing as I thought,' he added.

Brandon grinned and shrugged, placing his hot-barrelled rifle on the sled alongside the woman. 'Shall we go?' he said quietly.

Jake glanced at the woman; she was looking up at Brandon with a slightly dazed expression.

'Best take her back to the cabin, I'd say,' said Jake.

She shook her head quickly. 'Can't we rest for a while?' she whispered. 'I — I don't feel very well.'

Jake eyed her quizzically. His expression was not unkind, in spite of the dance she had led them. Then he glanced at Brandon. 'What about it, friend? I have another line camp yonder in the trees. We could get a meal and some sleep if the lady wants it.'

Brandon nodded. He very much wanted to find out some more about this reckless young woman. If they took her straight back to the other cabin, the chance might never come. 'Very well,' he said. 'We'll do that. I could use some coffee myself, come to think about it.'

Jake laid his rifle aside and took up the rawhide whip, cracking it in the air above the dogs. With the woman on the sled, Brandon and Jake loping along beside it, they set off once more, up through the forest by a different route to that by which they had come. Neither man spoke during the latter part of the journey.

Jake conned the team down a winding trail beneath dense dark pines. The foliage overhead was so thick that in places there was barely enough snow to carry the sled. The trail became steeper. Jake checked the team, shouting to the dogs. From the distance came the cry of wolves, long-drawn and mournful against the background of the otherwise silent forest. The woman lolled on the sled, furs drawn up round her face to keep out the bitter cold.

Then without any warning there was a sharp cracking noise above their heads. Jake gave a frantic yell, trying to drag the team aside. He was too late. The next instant a bough from one of the pines came crashing down, overburdened by snow, narrowly missing the backs of the team.

Brandon shouted a warning; Jake cursed and threw up his arm in self-defence. The snow-laden bough tipped over on end just as the woman looked upwards, aghast. Then it toppled sideways, settling across the body of the sled before the dogs could drag it clear.

Brandon had a fleeting glimpse of the woman's muffled white face before it was buried under black-green pine and powdered snow. Then the entire sled seemed to be overwhelmed as the dogs plunged and struggled to drag it forward.

Jake, on whose side the bough had fallen, staggered away, muttering to himself. There was snow in his beard, and his face was grim as Brandon hurled himself on the end of the bough and started to heave and strain to move it off the sled.

'Give me a hand!' Brandon said. 'This is hell!'

Jake needed no prodding. He was there at Brandon's side, struggling with all his might; but the bough was heavy and obstinate, and it was several minutes before they had lifted it clear and revealed the figure of the woman. Her head was hanging sideways at an angle.

'Neck's broken,' grunted Jake pessimistically.

But Brandon would have none of it. He knelt beside the sled and lifted her by the shoulders. There was just a chance, he thought desperately, hopefully. If the back uprights of the sled frame had taken the force of the fall, she might have escaped serious harm. He prayed that it would be so.

'Dead?' queried Jake in a whisper. He seemed awed, oddly helpless in the face of this disaster.

'No, not dead,' answered Brandon quietly. 'Can't tell how bad she is yet. The sled frame took most of it, I think. Can you ease the dogs forward?'

He was trying to decide what had happened to the woman as he talked. She was unconscious, but as yet he could not tell the reason. If it was a crack on the head, it might not be too bad; but a direct crash from the weight of the bough would be a different matter. It all depended . . .

Jake, obeying mechanically, stirred the frightened dogs into movement. The sled moved away.

'That's enough,' said Brandon. 'Now I can see what I'm doing.' He was loosening the furs round the woman, checking up on her. As far as he could tell under the circumstances, there was no spot at which she could have taken the full force of the bough; but a smudge of blood showed on her forehead. By raising the fur hood of her upper coat, he discovered a great wheal at the edge of the hairline. 'How far is this cabin of yours?' he demanded.

'Mile. Maybe less. What's the damage?'

'Not serious, I hope. Let's get on. Take it as easy as you can.'

The trapper nodded, cracking his whip and shouting to the dogs. The sled moved off.

Within fifteen minutes they had come within sight of the trap-line cabin. It nestled against a wooded shoulder of land, and in the gathering darkness had a snug look about it that cheered Brandon up considerably. What with the fight against the wolf pack and the woman's accident, he was anxious to reach some shelter. The second wave of the blizzard that Jake had foretold was sweeping down on them by this time. Visibility dropped so that they could barely see the cabin when they were less than fifty yards away from it. Snow was whipped in their faces by a driving wind that whined and whistled through the trees.

'Lucky we didn't try making the main place,' commented Brandon.

Jake merely grunted. The log-built cabin loomed up in front of them. He halted the team and turned the dogs loose while Brandon went across and got the cabin door open. Then he returned to the sled, which Jake had pushed into the lee of the cabin wall. Between them they lifted the woman and took her inside. A moment or two later Jake lit a lamp and shut out the storm. The inside of the cabin was cold and raw.

'Put her in the bunk, friend,' said Jake. 'I'll get a fire going.'

Brandon was already carrying the limp figure of the woman across to the wooden-sided bunk against the wall. The lamplight, a sickly yellow gleam, cast dizzying shadows before him. He lowered the woman onto the bunk and covered her with furs and blankets. She was breathing quite steadily, and some of the colour had returned to her cheeks.

The crackle of wood in the iron stove

was a welcome sound. Jake put a billy of water on to boil. 'Coffee soon,' he said tersely. 'There's a first-aid box on the shelf over yonder if you need it.'

'Thanks.' Brandon was watching the woman, his mind probing out in many directions. The first thing he wanted to know was who she was. Under a thick fur topcoat she wore a check lumber jacket and tough cord breeches. It did not take him long to search for clues to her identity; but the only things her pockets yielded were a somewhat soiled handkerchief, a packet of American cigarettes, a petrol lighter, and, finally and most important, a thin pigskin wallet. Brandon seized on it greedily. A glance over his shoulder showed him Jake busy at the stove. Turning away, he opened the wallet and sorted eagerly through the contents.

Warmth was beginning to seep through the air from the fire.

There was nothing in the wallet to give him any clue as to who the woman was. It was strangely barren of such things as driving licenses, letters or anything with a name — almost, he thought, as if the woman had gone out of her way to avoid bearing any identifying mark whatever. Which was queer in a way. Usually women carried a clutter of old letters, receipts and unpaid bills. But the only things here were a snapshot and a newspaper clipping.

The snapshot showed a broad-shouldered young man with a pipe in his mouth. What looked like fair hair ran back in a straight sweep from a high-domed fore-head. His mouth was wide and humorous, with a big moustache above it. He wore an open-necked shirt and dark-coloured shorts. In the background was the edge of a sun-drenched swimming pool, with palms on the far side of ruffled water. Scrawled across the lower half of the snapshot were the words: 'All my love. Nick.'

Brandon studied the snap, curiously aware that he knew the face in some now-forgotten connection. He turned his attention to the newspaper clipping in which it had been folded. The brief paragraph caused him to suck in his breath and glance at the woman. The clipping was taken from a local small-town news sheet. It bore no date line.

★   ★   ★

'The people of Frostville will be proud to learn of the appointment of Nicolas Shawn to an important post in the U.S. research station in northern Alaska. Shawn — Nick to his friends — was a well-known member of Frostville society before leaving this town to take up highly secret duties in the interests of the American people. We, the editorial staff, representing public feeling in Frostville, as always, wish him well in his latest appointment, which we know will bring even greater prestige on the graduates of our municipal college, in the classrooms of which Nick Shawn once studied.'

★   ★   ★

There was a little more in the same vein, and Brandon read it through with a quickening of his pulse as things began to fall into place in his mind. Nicolas Shawn

69

. . . So the woman had some connection to the missing scientist, did she? Or was he jumping to conclusions rather too quickly? Somehow he didn't think so.

The snapshot signed 'Nick' was undoubtedly of Shawn, and the very fact of its being in the woman's possession, together with the clipping, definitely pointed to friendship between them. Since the woman had acted so strangely, there was a chance, and a good one, that her very presence in these wild and barren places had its part in the scheme of things. Shawn was thought to have gone east after leaving Alaska. Did he have a rendezvous to keep with someone in these parts? With the woman perhaps? It was an intriguing question, and Brandon realised that if he was ever to find out for certain, he must act as cagily as he could. An open and direct accusation would be sure to make her cautious, shutting her up like a clam if she thought any of them guessed at her connection with the missing man. There must be more subtle ways of going about it, but just at the moment Brandon could not think of any. And the woman was still out for the count.

Carefully, he replaced the snapshot and clipping in the wallet, together with the other few odd scraps of paper. Then he put the wallet and her other belongings back in the pockets from which he had shamelessly taken them in the first place.

Jake had the coffee boiling on the stove. He shot a quizzical glance at Brandon as the latter stood up. Brandon had examined the woman more thoroughly by this time, and was certain in his own mind that apart from the crack on the head, she had received no serious injury. It was just a matter of time before she regained her senses.

'Find out who she is, friend?' asked Jake solemnly.

Brandon shook his head. 'No,' he replied. 'She doesn't carry any identifying things at all. Not directly, at any rate. It's a queer kettle of fish, Jake. Let's get some coffee inside her and see how she reacts.' He gave a cheerful grin.

Outside, the wind was getting stronger. Snow was packing against the small square window panes of the cabin. There was no light at all beyond the lamp. Wind howled in the stovepipe and chimney with a fierce insistence.

'Blizzard,' commented Jake, pouring coffee.

'Do they usually last long?' enquired Brandon. 'I'm more used to dust storms.'

Jake shrugged. 'May not stop for a week,' he said pessimistically. 'But this time of year you never can tell. By dawn it may have passed. We'll worry when the time comes, friend.'

'That's a fair enough attitude,' agreed Brandon; but he viewed with distaste the prospect of being cooped up in the cabin indefinitely. For one thing, he wanted to reach Great Bear Lake, and was still faced with the problem of what to do about the woman. With Jake in the picture, any solution would be made more difficult.

Jake filled the stove with wood, setting it roaring so the top glowed red. They took off their fur garments, glad to be rid of the weight and free to move about easily.

'How far is Great Bear from here?'

Brandon asked suddenly.

Jake glanced up at him. 'Near enough a couple of hundred miles,' he answered. 'You weren't thinking of going there, were you?'

Brandon smiled. 'Not right now,' he said. He took a mug of coffee from the trapper and laced it stiffly with whisky from a bottle on the table. Then, after testing its heat with his lips, he raised the woman's head and fed her a little.

The treatment proved a good one. Before many minutes were past, she stirred and opened her eyes, peering up at him blankly.

Brandon had washed and bound the wheal on her forehead. He let her rest a while without speaking, then gave her the mug of coffee to handle herself. She met his gaze, obviously at something of a loss for words.

'Don't worry,' he said gently. 'Just relax and leave things to us. We're snowed up at the moment in one of Jake's trap-line cabins. Remember the wolves . . . ? A tree came down on the sled and hit you. Nothing much.'

She nodded slowly, sipping coffee. 'I wasn't sure,' she murmured cryptically. Then she glanced at Jake. 'How far are we from Great Bear Lake?' she asked unexpectedly.

Jake didn't answer immediately. He shot a look at Brandon. Then: 'You two should get together,' he answered laconically. 'Seems you have something in common, at any rate. Great Bear Lake is too far to trek in weather like this, ma'am, so you forget it.'

The woman was staring at Brandon intently. Something in common? Her eyes were wary.

5

Human Storm

'Forget it . . . ?' mused Brandon quietly. 'Yes, Jake, you may be right.' He swung on the woman, suddenly smiling in his own most friendly fashion. 'What's your name?' he demanded. 'If we're going to be comrades in trouble, we should know each other better.'

She swallowed uneasily, still watching him with a hint of caution in her eyes. Then: 'I don't know where the trouble comes in,' she muttered. 'You don't seem to be worried.'

'I'm not,' Brandon answered with a shrug. 'But you still haven't answered my question. Or is your name a secret?' His smile tempered the persistence in his voice.

There was a definite challenge in her gaze at that. 'Of course not,' she answered. 'People usually call me Stephanie, Steve for short. Is that what you wanted to know?'

'Thank you ... Stephanie,' Brandon replied with a little bow. 'Stephanie what?'

'Smith,' she said without hesitation. 'Original, isn't it?'

Brandon had to be content with that. For the moment he thought he had pressed her far enough. And Jake was taking a deeper interest in the pair of them than Brandon altogether fancied. Jake was a first-rate person, but there were elements in this affair that were outside the trapper's scope.

'More coffee?' said Brandon, changing the subject abruptly.

Stephanie accepted with a grave little smile. 'You're being kinder than I deserve,' she said. 'I've never thanked you for what you did a while ago. I suppose Elko was killed, wasn't he? I'd have ended the same way if it hadn't been for you two.'

'It would have been touch and go,' admitted Brandon. 'I should try to forget it if I were you. Get some sleep if you can. Great Bear Lake won't shift, and none of us can possibly leave this cabin while the storm lasts.' He paused. 'That's something beyond our control, Steve, so you might as well accept it.' He grinned.

She sighed deeply, putting a hand to the bandage on her head and wincing slightly. She said nothing more, but drained her mug and lay back in the bunk.

Brandon exchanged a glance with Jake. The latter gave a shrug as if to say he didn't understand women and didn't particularly want to. Silence fell in the cabin, broken by the howling of the wind outside. Brandon smoked a pipe of tobacco. Jake rolled himself up in his blankets and went to sleep.

The blizzard had an isolating effect on Brandon's mind. It was as if he was living temporarily in another world, cut off from the things he knew and the lives of other people. He looked at Stephanie. Her eyes were closed. With a queer detachment, he thought back to the moment in which he and Henri and Ramshorn had arrived at the other cabin. The place had looked safe and secure, with its short chimney, its lean-to pelt store, and its wood pile, snow-covered. The inside had been much the same as it was here, only larger and roomier.

There was a pattern to life in these parts, he reflected solemnly. A pattern that was woven from death and the threat of death, and the struggle for existence against the perils of the wild. He remembered the ravening wolf pack; the mortal cry of fear that had reached his ears when the pack got Elko down and tore him to pieces. Yes, he thought, it was a pattern all right. Much the same pattern as he had found in other parts of the world where might was right and the weakest perished. And he was pitted against it himself now. So, apparently, was Stephanie Smith — if Smith was her real name, which he doubted.

Smith and Shawn . . . Shawn on his way east from Alaska . . . Going to Great Bear Lake? But Brandon himself was bound for that locality. And so was she. And she was linked irrevocably with Shawn. All the aspects of the pattern were directed at Great Bear. With what object?

That was the question that kept confronting him. Was this woman, this Steve Smith, a bad hat? He looked at her sleeping profile again and could not bring himself to believe it. Yet there were times when she behaved as if she was. The warmth of the cabin made him drowsy. He knocked out his pipe and went to sleep.

The long night came slowly to an end. With the lifting of darkness, the trio in the cabin stirred and woke; first Jake, then Brandon, and finally Stephanie.

Brandon's first act was to look outside, finding to his intense relief that the blizzard had blown itself out and that everywhere was peace and stillness in a snowbound scene among the towering pines.

The trapper joined him at the door, looking out over his shoulder and nodding in a satisfied manner. 'We move today,' he said.

Brandon thought swiftly. He did not want to break with Jake, who had been a good friend; but he definitely did not wish to return to the cabin where Henri and

Ramshorn were waiting. 'If I made it worth your while, would you take us on to Great Bear Lake?' he said. 'It's important that I get there, and going back won't help at all. What about it?'

Jake stood perfectly still, staring out at the snow. 'Long way. You'd be a fool to try it, and I'd be a fool to risk my life and my dogs for a woman. It is because of her that you want to carry on.' His voice was flat.

Brandon glanced at him shrewdly. 'Not altogether,' he said, speaking in a low tone. 'I *do* have to get there. If she wants to go along, all well and good. I don't object.'

'I do.' Jake's voice was harder. 'You be sensible and come back with me. I'll take you on to Dawson as soon as spring breaks fair. Then you can get another plane to Great Bear Lake if you want to. Anyway, that's my answer, friend, and you can take it or leave it.'

Brandon was faced with an awkward decision. For the moment he put it off and went back to wondering about Stephanie. 'Let's rustle up breakfast,' he said. Jake merely nodded, not pursuing the conversation further.

They went back indoors to find Stephanie awake. Her head, she informed Brandon, was aching a bit, but otherwise she was feeling no ill effects. Brandon told her the weather had cleared. She brightened up considerably, then seemed to realise that it would mean a return to the main cabin and the total frustration of her plans. Her face fell almost comically. She made an excuse and went outside the cabin, standing for a moment in the deep snow that was piled in front of the door.

Jake called out: 'Don't think of taking my team, ma'am.'

She turned her head and glared at him, but said not a word.

Brandon eyed Jake in a speculative manner. The man's remark had put a fresh idea into his head. 'Sell me your team,' he said. 'Any price you name.'

The trapper's face went stiff, bearded jaw thrust out. 'Listen, mister,' he said, 'them huskies are my living. I wouldn't part with 'em for anything, understand? If you don't come back with me you can stay where you are, but you don't get the dogs under any circumstances.'

Brandon had guessed what the answer would be before it was given. He shrugged, beaten for once in his life.

Jake gave a curt nod, picking up an axe from against the wall and making for the door. 'I'll get some wood,' he said over his shoulder. 'You'll find food in the cupboard.'

'Right,' said Brandon.

Stephanie returned a few moments later. Jake disappeared somewhere round the end of the cabin. They heard the keen ring of his axe as he went to work.

Brandon looked at her and grinned. 'We might as well get on with the breakfast,' he said.

She nodded. It seemed as if she meant to accept the position with as much grace as possible. The inside of the cabin was warm. Brandon, setting a pan on the stove, took his jacket off. Clad in breeches, boots and his own beloved bush shirt with its tattered sleeves, he made a striking figure in the primitive setting of the cabin. At his belt hung the big revolver, without which he never ventured far beyond the fringe of civilisation.

Glancing in Stephanie's direction, he saw she was watching him with something like admiration. He turned away quickly. She was moving about, setting things on the table. But she did not speak.

'You still want to go to Great Bear?' he said presently. The clang and ring of Jake's axe were clearly audible from outside the cabin.

Stephanie was silent for a brief moment. Then: 'Yes,' she said quietly. 'Do you?'

'Uh-huh. Reach me down one of those tins, will you?'

She went to the cupboard. Beans. She stood on tiptoe, straining to the limit of her reach. Brandon grinned and did the job himself.

'Forgot you weren't all that tall,' he said apologetically. She turned to face him. Brandon held the tin of beans. They both looked down at it.

'What are we going to do?' she asked. 'Can't you buy his team?'

'He won't sell, and we can't just take it.

I think it's best to go back and try to repair the plane. Probably be quicker in the long run.'

'But suppose it isn't? It may be too late by then . . . ' She was speaking half to herself.

He watched her closely. 'Why are you so anxious?' he asked.

Before she could answer — if she meant to — the ringing of Jake's axe stopped abruptly. A scream of fear and pain took its place.

Brandon pivoted, dropping the beans on the table as he raced for the door. It took him only a second to reach the corner of the cabin. When he did so he sucked in his breath, drawing his revolver and diving forward with even greater urgency.

'Help!' Jake's strangled plea struck his eardrums loudly. There was stark panic in the shout.

The trapper was wrestling with an enormous shaggy-coated grizzly bear. The ponderous beast towered over him, jaws open, hot and steaming in the freezing air. Mighty claws dug into Jake's back as he struggled to force the animal off.

Brandon stopped in his tracks when only a few feet from the dreadful scene. His revolver bellowed, smashing a shot clean into the grizzly's face. But at the same time the bear gave a terrific heave, and Brandon heard the crunch of the trapper's spine as it broke. Then the grizzly grunted in a mixture of pain and perplexity as another of Brandon's bullets struck home. Jake's body sagged in the creature's weakening grasp, till the bear let it drop to the ground, where it lay quite still. Brandon aimed again, squeezing the trigger carefully. Before he could fire, he heard a cry of warning from Stephanie in the doorway of the cabin. The wounded bear was coming slowly towards him now, growling and grunting angrily. But it was almost on its last legs. Why had she shouted out?

The next instant she called again: 'Behind you! Look out!' Her voice was a sudden scream.

Brandon fired again at Jake's wounded killer. Then he swung round in time to feel the deadly embrace and the reeking breath of a second grizzly. The first beast was swaying drunkenly about, still struggling to live and reach the man who had wounded it. But Brandon himself had no time to watch it. He was plunged in a life-and-death struggle on his own account. The animal that had stolen up to his rear was a massive she-bear, fully seven feet in height as it overshadowed him.

A terrible fear gripped his heart. The sound of Jake's spine being broken still lingered in his mind. And he knew that there were only two shots left in his revolver. By sheer physical strength, he forced himself backwards in the clasp of the fearful fore-paws of the bear, bringing his gun up as he did so. He buried his fingers in the tangled fur of the creature's throat. Slowly but surely he was being hugged closer and closer to the animal's chest. Then he fired at point-blank range, straight into the open mouth of the bear.

The concussion almost knocked the beast over. For one instant Brandon thought he had failed. He fired again, his last remaining bullet in the gun. All the breath seemed to be squeezed from his lungs by the frightful pressure of those great encircling arms.

There was blood pouring from the bear's jaws, running down over its throat and his arm, soaking the front of his shirt in a warm flood. He tried with the strength of desperation to break the dying animal's grip, but muscular contraction only strengthened its tenacity.

And again he thought of Jake.

Smashing at the bear's head with the empty revolver, he managed to loosen its grasp a little. It was dying fast, but just then it looked as if it meant to crush Brandon to death in its mortal struggles.

Suddenly it staggered to one side, falling in a heap on the blood-stained snow, all life drained from its mighty carcase. Only in the nick of time did Brandon wrench himself clear, his clothes torn and splashed with crimson. Then the dead beast rolled over sideways, its weight enough to crush the breath out of any man. Brandon staggered away, his chest heaving as he gasped for air.

It was then that he caught sight of the

other grizzly. It was coming for him, mortally wounded, but growling in a horrible fashion. How it still possessed the vitality to stand after the wounds it had received he did not know, but it was plainly determined to avenge its mate. Brandon was now unarmed, and the bear was so close that its hot breath fanned his cheek. He turned and tried to run, but floundered and fell in the drifted snow. *This is it*, he thought.

The staccato crash of a rifle cut his mind in half. He looked up, dazed. The bulk of the bear was tottering above him. With a grab at life he rolled over, saving himself as the body of the grizzly came crashing down on the snow, landing inches from where he had been but a second before.

He lay still, panting, too overwhelmed by relief and temporary exhaustion to rise. Then he forced himself up as the bitter cold of the snow penetrated his clothing. He felt weak. Stephanie, of course, had killed the bear. In a way he owed his life to her; yet it was through her perversity that they were where they were at this moment. He thought of Jake, and a chill anger filled his mind.

The fight with the bear had brought him round to the front of the cabin. Stephanie was in the doorway, a smoking rifle in her hands. The line of her mouth was grim.

Brandon rose to his feet, going towards her slowly, still thinking of Jake. 'Thanks for that,' he said bleakly.

But her gaze was mutinous. The rifle stiffened in her grasp. She was covering him with it! It was a fact that only sank in on Brandon's mind by slow degrees. When it did, he came to a halt, watching her through narrowed eyes.

'Breakfast,' he said. 'Aren't you hungry?'

'I'll breakfast on the way to Great Bear,' she snapped. 'You and Jake can get the dog team harnessed up. I'm leaving!'

He could scarcely believe his ears. 'You're out of your mind,' he said hoarsely. He started towards her again, moving slowly. Would she really dare to shoot him? He doubted it.

'No!' she said quickly. 'Don't come any closer, please. I'm desperate, don't you understand?' Her eyes were blazing. 'Tell Jake to fix his dogs up. There's nothing you can do about it.'

Brandon stopped. She didn't know what had happened to Jake, he thought incredulously. 'Tell Jake yourself!' he retorted coldly. 'I'll walk in front of you, *Miss Smith*!' He turned his back on her, striding through the snow to the corner of the cabin. He halted there. 'Go on,' he said in an icy tone. 'Give your orders.'

He could sense that she was close behind him. Then he heard the catch in her breath as she caught sight of the dead man's body, twisted grotesquely where it lay in the snow. Jake had his face to the grey sky, eyes wide open, staring hideously. His mouth was open, too, the big white teeth bared in a grin of death. Frost hoared his beard, but there was no mist of breath above his bloodless lips.

Brandon turned then. His fingers closed on Stephanie's rifle and took it from her nerveless grasp. She offered no resistance. Only with difficulty did she tear her gaze from the dead body of the trapper. Then her head came round, and

90

her eyes met those of Brandon.

'Oh God!' she whispered. 'I didn't know. I swear I didn't!' There was panic close to the surface now.

'We'd better go inside,' said Brandon. He tucked the rifle under his arm, taking her by the elbow and urging her back through the snow.

Once inside the cabin, she broke loose and threw herself down on the bunk, burying her face in her hands. Brandon let her be and went on preparing a meal as if nothing had happened. This, he thought sourly, ought to teach her a lesson. He had an idea that she was already suffering pangs of remorse. A few more wouldn't do any harm.

'Pull yourself together!' he said harshly. 'It won't bring him back to life if you snivel in a corner. Come and eat!' He spoke brutally on purpose, hoping to anger her.

She raised her head. 'I wasn't snivelling,' she said. 'I know it's my fault he was killed. But you don't know what's behind it all. You couldn't, or you'd never blame me for doing all I can to reach the place where I'm going.'

Brandon eyed her stonily. This was better, he thought. 'Come and have your breakfast,' he said. 'We'll bury him afterwards. There are several things you and I have got to understand. The first is to know where we stand — and where we're going. Coffee?'

6

Greedy River

She came across to the table and sat down on the edge of a wooden chair, her back to the heat of the stove. Her face was pale and suddenly old. Brandon pushed a mug of steaming coffee towards her. She murmured her thanks, studiously avoiding his gaze. He put food in front of her. She looked up then. The bandage on her head was twisted askew, maize-coloured hair poking out from beneath it. She brushed it off her forehead.

'Jake was killed because I ran out back at the other cabin,' she said clearly. 'But I had to, don't you understand? And you saved my life when the wolves chased us. Elko died because of me, too. What do you think that makes me feel like?'

'A heel, Steve; but maybe I wouldn't blame you so much if I knew a little more about the circumstances.' Brandon started

93

eating his food. The cabin door was open, pale daylight entering, though the lamp was still alight on the table. The chill of the outer air swept in and set the lamp flame dithering. Stephanie got up and closed the door with a shiver.

'I *am* a heel,' she said flatly. 'But I've got to reach Great Bear Lake as soon as I can.'

Brandon raised his eyes as she sat down opposite him. 'Why?' There was little compromise in his tone. She did not answer, but toyed with her food in a listless fashion.

'Why?' repeated Brandon. 'Because of Nicolas Shawn . . . ?'

All the colour drained from her cheeks as she stared at him. Then she suddenly laughed. It was a cracked, unpleasant sound. *She's still close to being scared*, Brandon thought.

'Nicolas Shawn?' she echoed. 'Who's he?'

Brandon eyed her sceptically, shaking his head. 'Not good enough!' he said firmly. 'You wanted the radio switched off when Shawn was mentioned in a newscast. Or is your memory so short you've forgotten?'

'Oh, that . . . I had a headache. I wasn't listening.'

'Now look here,' said Brandon quietly, laying down his fork and propping his elbows on the edge of the table. 'Didn't I say we'd have to understand each other? I've had about enough of this fencing. You want to go to Great Bear Lake. So do I. But the difference between us is that you're mixed up with Shawn in some way. I want to know about it or we don't move from where we are.'

She looked at him apprehensively. 'Are you threatening me?' she demanded coldly. 'How can you stop me from doing what I have to do? You wouldn't have the nerve to use force on a woman. I know your kind. You're much too gallant!'

Brandon grinned. 'Thanks,' he replied. 'But I'm not quite sure if it's meant as a compliment or not. However, to continue, let me make it quite plain that I will not hesitate to use any means I think fit to prevent you running out on me. On the other hand, if you're sensible, we can come to some arrangement. Wouldn't that be better?'

She sighed. 'I see what you mean,' she said quietly. 'Look, if you had a sister whose life was in danger, would you let anything stand in your way of going to save her? That's my position; and whether you like it or not, that's all I intend to tell you. I don't know you well, and I don't particularly want to; but if you'll trust me that far, I'll do the same. *I* don't want to know your reasons for going to Great Bear.'

Brandon smiled and shrugged. 'They aren't mysterious,' he volunteered. 'I'm due to join a scientific prospecting party. It's led by Hans Vetjek, an old friend of mine. If I don't get there soon, I'll miss half the fun.'

She was staring at him curiously, almost suspiciously. Then she pulled herself together and blinked owlishly. 'So will I,' she said unexpectedly. 'All right, my friend. I don't want to know your business. But I still have to reach Great Bear. Because of ... my sister, you understand. Are you satisfied now?' She was watching him anxiously.

Brandon raised a smile. 'Only partly,' he admitted, 'but I'd be a boor to ask further after such a denial.' The sister angle, he decided, was eyewash. Great Bear Lake was not the kind of vicinity in which women like Stephanie had a sister lurking. It was Shawn behind this business, without a doubt. And if Shawn was up to no good when he disappeared from the U.S. base in Alaska, then it looked as if the woman was aiding and abetting him. A serious position, putting Brandon on the wrong side of the fence if he did nothing about it.

'Thank you for that at any rate,' said Stephanie slowly. 'Can we work as friends, then? How soon can we leave here?'

Brandon went on with his breakfast. 'I'll see to poor old Jake when I'm through,' he said. 'You can pack the gear and hunt round for ammunition and stores. We've a long way to go, don't forget.'

Her obvious relief was almost pitiful to see. Brandon pushed his plate aside and rose to his feet, looking round the cabin for a spade or pick. Stephanie collected things they might need. Brandon found what he wanted and went outside, speaking to the dogs as he passed. The leader of the team, Baron, nuzzled his hand. They wanted feeding, he remembered.

Jake's body lay where it had fallen. He shovelled away the snow and used a pick to dig a shallow grave in the frozen earth. The exercise made him sweat. When the grave was dug, he dragged the trapper's body over and settled it in, covering the man's gaunt face with the fur of his hood. Then he stood up, aware of Stephanie at his side. He glanced at her solemnly.

'He lived and died in the wilds he loved,' she whispered.

Brandon shovelled snow in silence. They returned to the cabin. She had already found food for the dogs, to which Brandon added strips of raw meat cut from the two dead grizzlies. The dogs ate ravenously.

Inside the cabin, Brandon looked round. 'Well,' he began, 'we can go back and chance the plane being repaired, or we can push on overland. The first is the more sensible alternative.'

She frowned. 'If it doesn't come off, we'll waste so much time,' she protested. 'You're good enough at this kind of thing to get through by dog team, aren't you?'

'Maybe.'

Her eyes were pleading. 'Then please, let's risk it!'

They camped that night on a high wind-swept plateau. Firelight gave an illusion of warmth, but little more. The distant moan of timber wolves brought a shudder from Stephanie, but nevertheless she insisted on taking her turn on guard.

'You trust me enough for that, don't you?' she said in a challenging manner.

Brandon grinned. 'I think so,' he replied. 'I'll wake you in a couple of hours. Get some sleep now.'

She huddled down on the sled, buried in furs. Time passed. Brandon kept the fire going; its blaze made him forget some of the cold. Before his two hours were up, however, Stephanie had come to his side, shivering.

'I can't sleep in this cold,' she whispered.

They crouched by the fire, as close to its narrow warmth as they could get. Brandon piled more furs round her shoulders. 'It'll be just as cold at Great Bear,' he told her.

'That's different. You're still trying to dig out secrets, aren't you?' There was no rancour in her tone.

'I'm curious,' he admitted.

She drew closer to him, seeking warmth. When she spoke again, her voice was so low that he could barely hear what she said. 'How did you know — ? That is . . . what made you think I had anything to do with Nicolas Shawn?'

Brandon hesitated for a moment. Then he told her about the wallet, the snapshot, the clipping. 'Shawn's a friend of yours, isn't he? Why don't you be honest with me, Steve?'

She did not reply at once. 'Please,' she said. 'It's not my own business. I know what you're thinking, but you're wrong.'

'I hope I am,' he said, disappointed by her lack of faith. She said no more, falling into fitful slumber, curled up in the crook of his body like a child. He made no attempt to wake her.

* * *

It was not until four days later that they sighted the Mackenzie River. Darkness was falling. Brandon drove the dogs towards it, seeking a sheltered spot for the night. Away to the left of the line they were following were dense thickets of pine and fir, dark against the growing darkness. He swung the team towards them, finally halting in the gloom of a standing clump of timber that abutted the river bank.

'Wood, food, and a fire, Steve!' he said. 'We're more than halfway to Great Bear now.'

She sighed, yawned and stretched, then busied herself.

Since the beginning of the trek, Brandon had had no cause to find fault with Stephanie as a travelling companion. But in spite of their strengthening friendship, he had learnt nothing more about her private affairs. Because of some tacit understanding between them, he did not question her. Even had he done so, he knew it would not solve the problems on his mind. And now there was the river to cross. Not a simple undertaking.

They were barely settled in before he made an excuse and walked down through the trees to the edge of the river bank. He stood there, hands on his hips, staring out at the cold, white luminous surface. It groaned and creaked. He could almost visualise it heaving sluggishly, the water underneath flowing swift and dark. Greedy river. The cold seeped in through his heavy clothing. He turned on his heel and went back to the fire.

Stephanie was kneeling beside it. She looked up as he came to a halt, smiling cheerfully at him. The reddish glow of the fire was reflected on her face. Part of the fur hood dropped back off her hair, leaving it free to absorb the light of the flames in sudden glory.

Brandon swallowed hard. She made a very lovely picture just then. He found himself hoping that she wasn't nixed up in anything unsavoury. But Nicolas Shawn ... He thrust the thought from his mind.

'How are grub stakes, Steve?' he asked gaily.

'Won't be long,' she told him, brushing hair from her forehead with a sweeping gesture of her hand. There was a tantalising quality in her smile that affected him when he least expected it. He remembered the river.

'Is it quite so cold?' she said presently. 'Or is it my imagination?'

Brandon shrugged. 'I'm frozen. Must be your imagination.' But he knew she was right. There was a raw, damp quality in the night air now. And the river ... 'We must move before dawn,' he said. 'It'll take time to cross.'

She nodded. 'Wake me early.'

They settled for the night, huddled together in a nest of furs, the firelight playing on their faces. Brandon stole an hour's sleep, leaving Stephanie to watch. Then she slumbered and he stayed awake. Her head was cradled in the bend of his arm. The rifle lay across his knees.

With plenty of wood to hand, and the eerie creak and grind of the river ice for company, the hours passed.

By the time night was halfway through, the cold had become intense. Brandon heaved a sigh of genuine relief. It was freezing hard, there was no doubt about it. If they wasted no time in getting across, all would be well.

Gradually the sound of ice ceased altogether. Stephanie moved restlessly against him. He glanced down at her upturned face. Her eyes were closed. There was an odd little quirk at the corner of her mouth — a red, inviting mouth. Brandon drew the furs up around her and thought about other things.

She was awake long before daybreak. They ate and packed in silence. The river was quiet: a rough, uneven stretch of ice about a hundred yards in width. It would not be a simple feat to get the sled across, but they must do it somehow.

'Ready?' he said with a hint of grimness.

Stephanie nodded. They set off, skirting the river bank for nearly a quarter of a mile before finding a place that offered easy access to the surface of broken ice. It was barely light, and the air seemed to freeze in their lungs as they breathed.

The dogs whined and yapped as they started across the ice. Both Brandon and Stephanie had to walk, guiding the sled over patches of rough. The dogs strained and struggled in the traces. Brandon's anxiety increased the further out on the ice they were. He could feel it creaking under his feet, and a sidelong glance at his companion showed her face pale and drawn. She understood without him telling her.

They were almost in the middle of the river by now. It had taken a full fifteen minutes to get that far. Brandon heaved at the sled, shouting to the dogs. The sled was caught in a crevice, demanding the strength of both him and Stephanie to free it. An ominous crack sounded sharply in the air from somewhere ahead.

'It's breaking up, isn't it?' said Stephanie.

Brandon nodded grimly. 'We'll make it,' he said.

A clear run of several yards opened up

ahead. Brandon used the long team whip, cracking it in the air above the dogs. They strained forward eagerly, as if realising the peril of being caught on the ice in the event of a break-up.

Stephanie stayed close to Brandon, struggling with the sled. The ice was broken and rough, so that the steel-shod runners ground and slithered groaningly. Suddenly Brandon swore, shouting to the dogs and swerving them to one side. A still patch of icy black water opened up just in front. The sled came round, skirting the water patch narrowly.

But more was to come. No sooner were they clear of one danger before another showed itself. There were definite signs of a rapid break-up now. Brandon paused for breath and stared round with growing desperation. There were breaks in the ice on all sides. If they did get across, it would be a miracle.

The very ice on which they stood was shivering. Stephanie gripped his arm fearfully. 'We'll never make it,' she breathed. 'Oh, Rex . . .'

'Chin up!' he snapped. His jaw was

thrust out defiantly. Once more he started the team. The dogs were plainly afraid. Their hackles rose, and several of them whimpered, tails curled tightly between their legs.

'Mush! Mush!' yelled Brandon. The sled moved off, crossing a patch of solid ice, only to be brought up short a moment later by a gradually widening channel. Brandon gave a muttered curse, his eyes seeking some fresh way. The sled came round again, retracing the marks of its own runners. Then he swerved it aside, gaining a yard or two, forcing the dogs to leap a gradually widening crevice. The grinding and rubbing of the breaking ice was deafening now. It broke and reared all round them. Stephanie's face was a white mask of fear. Brandon himself thought the end was close.

A few minutes later he knew it could not go on. Another abortive attempt was foiled by the breaking ice. When he turned back again, it was only to find that a fresh break was showing in their path.

'Rex!' gasped Stephanie. 'Look! We're cut off!'

His mouth hardened. There was water on all sides of their position. They were trapped on dangerous floating ice only a little more than halfway across the Mackenzie. 'We'll have to stop where we are till it piles against more,' he said grimly. 'Be ready for a dash, kid.'

Their ice floe ground against its neighbour, a great lump breaking off and bobbing sluggishly in the dark water. But before Brandon could take the sled to the point of impact, the gap had widened again. A man might jump, but a dog team would never make it.

In the cold grey daylight, they stared about them, looking death in the face and knowing it for what it was.

The floe drifted close to a large, solid-looking patch. Brandon whipped up the team and raced for the join. There was a splintering crack to the rear just as they reached the meeting of ice. The ice reared up beneath their feet, but the leading dogs were already across the gap. Brandon grabbed at Stephanie, then felt himself slithering backwards towards a jagged, grinding mill of shattered ice. He held his breath, not daring to look. Suddenly the floe tilted forward again, pivoting drunkenly as it wallowed in the freezing water.

Brandon kept his grip on Stephanie, then scrambled to his feet on the pitching surface of the ice. There was no sign of the sled or the dogs. They'd been caught and dragged under when the floe tipped up — gone, finished in an instant. 'Come on!' he snapped urgently. 'Run for it!'

They raced for the edge of the floe, jumping to its bigger neighbour. Landing safely, he dragged her to her feet and started running fast for the next gap. Without the sled and the team to encumber them, they stood a chance, albeit a desperate one.

Leaping from floe to floe, sometimes going back, sprawling and floundering as they went, they gradually cheated death. Sweat was running down Brandon's back in spite of the cold, and Stephanie was gasping for breath as she staggered along at his side. Only the greedy jaws of breaking ice and the strong sense of self-preservation in their minds kept them going.

They were ten yards from the river bank now, with broken ice to cross before reaching safety. Stephanie fell on her face, to be dragged upright by Brandon with almost brutal force. He was driving her as much as leading her, for every second wasted was a threat to their lives. Water, black and cold, lapped at their feet as a floe tipped and sent them skittering backwards. Brandon saw a chance and seized it. Taking Stephanie by the hand, he balanced himself precariously. The ice was sloping at a dangerous angle.

'Jump for that!' he said.

They leapt outwards and downwards, landing heavily on another piece of ice, picking themselves up quickly, going on to the next and the next till the bank was only one leap away. Stephanie fell again, to be lifted up bodily by Brandon for the last wild jump. How they made it he never knew, for when he looked back from the frozen snow of the bank there was a ten-yard gap between it and the nearest ice floe. It must have opened as they jumped, and the whole of the river was now one tumbled mass of jagged blocks, themselves alive with some hidden momentum as they piled one on top of another, broken and driven and carried by the current. Brandon closed his eyes briefly, trying to steady the pounding of his heart. Stephanie was nearly exhausted, and he himself could not have carried on much further.

Presently she sat up. Her chest was still heaving painfully. There was a bitterness about her mouth that made him realise the gravity of their position. The dogs were gone, together with all their stores and weather protection. All they had saved was one rifle that he carried slung, and his own revolver.

They exchanged a glance of understanding, then Brandon smiled. It was not an easy smile.

7

The Stranger

Stephanie shuddered uncontrollably. 'What are we going to do?' she said in a small, troubled voice.

Brandon felt inside his furs for a cigarette and offered her one. 'Sorry they aren't American,' he said, grinning.

She stared at him, puzzled for a moment, then chuckled. 'I forgot you'd been through my pockets,' she said with a tinge of maliciousness. 'Not that it matters now. Nothing matters a lot.' Her voice trailed away in dejection.

Brandon lit her cigarette for her. He must keep her spirits up at all costs, he thought. There was plenty of trouble ahead, and they were ill-equipped to face it. 'We'd better find a more sheltered spot than this,' he said. Action — that was the thing. They must keep on the move.

Stephanie rose reluctantly. 'I'm tired

and fed up,' she complained. 'We can't possibly get through to Great Bear now, with no dogs or food! It must be a good hundred miles, Rex.'

'Now look,' he said gently, 'we aren't beaten by a long chalk, so perk up for heaven's sake, there's a good kid. If we can find a spot to rest up for a few hours I can shoot some food, even if it's only a tree-rat!'

She eyed him speculatively. 'You know,' she murmured, 'the more I get to know you, the more I admire you. That may be an odd thing to say, but I'm honest about it. Doesn't matter what happens, you always have an answer. You must be one of the few real optimists in the world, I think.'

Brandon grinned. 'I try,' he said quietly. 'Come along now.'

She shook her head doubtfully. They started off, side by side, knee-deep in loose snow that hindered them badly. Brandon was striking up the slope above the river bank. There were trees and bare rocks showing higher up, dark against the glistening white and blue of ice and snow.

He wondered if he would find anything to shoot for food. But the first consideration was a fire. Nothing like a fire for raising morale.

Presently Stephanie said: 'I don't think it's much use, Rex. In spite of your optimism, we'll never get to Great Bear in time — even if we make it at all.'

He glanced at her obliquely, wondering if he would learn anything now that she thought they were beaten. It might be worthwhile fostering the idea a little. 'It'll take time, of course,' he admitted. 'Why is time so important, Steve? Does it make all that difference?'

She nodded slowly, then grabbed at his arm to save herself from plunging into an unexpected drift. Without snowshoes, they both found it tricky going. 'It's a sort of race against time,' she said.

'Why? Because of your sister?'

But she was silent, shaking her head obstinately. Brandon plodded on, keeping his eyes about him in the hope of a snap shot with the rifle at anything that moved. But the locality seemed devoid of wildlife. They were in among the broken ground now, treacherous going, with drifts, overhangs of frozen snow; pitfalls of every kind. But a few moments later he decided it was worth it. They were suddenly confronted by an enormous overhang of glistening snow. The palest hint of sunlight caught it brightly, reflecting back on bare yellowish rock where the wind had whipped it clean of snow. And underneath the snow of the overhang was a cave in the rocks. It was a poor sort of cave admittedly, no more than five or six feet in depth, but to Brandon and Stephanie it had a sheltered, cosy appearance. Despite the thaw it was bitterly cold, and they were glad to get inside for a while.

'I'll get some wood and leave you with a fire,' he said. 'Then I'll see what people live on in these parts.'

She did not answer his smile. Instead she unfastened her furs and brought a tin from an inner pocket. 'Have some beans before you go,' she said. 'Don't know what made me do it, but I put a couple of these in my pocket before we left.'

Brandon grinned his appreciation.

'Bless you for that at any rate!' he said. 'Here, I'll get a fire going.'

'It's wonderful,' she said a few minutes later, 'what one tin of beans and a fire can do.'

He looked across the cave. She was sitting hunched up against the wall, furs drawn round her. Smoke stung her eyes and made them red, yet her expression was almost content.

'Have some more warm water,' he offered. 'They say it's good for digestion.' He tried to joke, but she did not respond.

Presently she said: 'You've been very patient, Rex. So patient that now I'm going to talk a little more freely. By the time we get to Great Bear Lake it won't matter, but at least I owe you some kind of explanation.' She broke off, turning sombre eyes on him.

He filled his pipe and lit it with a brand from the fire. 'Don't feel that sort of obligation,' he told her gently. 'I admit I'm curious, but I gave up demanding explanations long ago.'

She nodded. 'I know that, which is possibly why I'm willing to tell you a certain amount. I can't tell you everything, you understand. Even if we both died out here in the wilds, it wouldn't be fair.'

'We won't die,' he said. 'Carry on.'

'I'm an American,' she told him. 'My name isn't really Smith. I lied when I told you that.'

Brandon smiled and nodded. 'I guessed as much. What is your name?'

'Olsbert,' she answered. 'Stephanie Olsbert.' She paused, giving Brandon an opening.

'Olsbert . . . ?' he echoed, frowning. 'And your sister, if I'm not mistaken, is Ingrid. Right?'

She caught her breath in surprise. 'How — how did you know?' she demanded blankly.

Brandon chuckled. 'Isn't Ingrid a member of the party I'm supposed to join when I get to Great Bear? I have a list of the names somewhere. There are seven in the party, including myself, the absentee. But tell me, where does Ingrid come into the picture? Mind, I've never met her. All I know is that she holds a degree in minerology, was recommended by a board in Washington to join Vetjek's party, and that her special line is sulphur research.' He broke off with a grin. 'Case history!' he added.

Stephanie gave him a shrewd and calculating look. 'You think you know it all,' she said. 'You're quite correct as far as it goes. But it doesn't go all the way, Rex. Ingrid has another side to her character as well as the one you detailed.'

'And that is?' He drew on his pipe, apparently unconcerned, but inwardly keyed up with excitement.

'You've heard of the witch-hunt phobia that's been prevalent in the United States recently over foreign spies?'

Brandon nodded. 'Who hasn't? Is Ingrid a spy?'

Stephanie gave a faint smile. 'It depends which way you look at it. The Espionage Section of the F.B.I. knows all about her, if that's what you mean. She's one of their operatives.'

'After witches in the frozen north? Or missing atom men from Alaska?' Brandon threw up his hands. 'And to think, Steve, that all this goes on in peaceful Canada. I suppose you're a member of some dangerous foreign agency?'

She smiled. 'You don't believe me, do you?'

He was serious at once. 'Yes,' he replied. 'I believe you, Steve. I was only trying to lighten the gloom. So Ingrid is a counter-espionage agent, is that it? May I enquire what she's countering in Canada?'

She met his gaze uneasily. 'I can't tell you that,' she replied after a moment's pause. 'All I can say is that her activities are not directed against Canadian interests.'

'I should hope not! But why are you going to join her? You said her life was in danger. That's a common thing in the spy game, isn't it?' He did not add that he himself had been a member of the most famous espionage system in the world at one time. All the old professional instincts were aroused by what she was telling him. But she was cagey, and even under the present circumstances was keeping back a great deal she might have added. He could sense that much.

'I suppose it is,' she murmured doubtfully. 'But you see, Rex, this is different. If I don't warn her, it'll be the end.' She leant towards him earnestly, her breath a milky, frosty steam in the cold air between them. 'I know something she doesn't know; something that endangers her life every minute till she's put on her guard.'

Brandon had never seen her small features so intensely grave before. He felt suddenly sorry for her. 'What is it you know?' he asked gently. 'Can't you share it with me?'

She hesitated for only a moment or two. Then: 'There's a man in that prospecting party. He isn't what he seems, and he isn't the man he's supposed to be. All his efforts are directed against both Canada and the U.S.A. In fact, he's an alien of the most dangerous type.'

Brandon leant forward. The fire crackled unheeded on the snow at the cave mouth. Further off they could hear the incessant clamour of the thawing river ice breaking up. It was cruel-sounding music in the crisp air.

'How do you know all this?' he asked quietly. 'If it's official information, why didn't Washington get in touch with your sister through Canadian channels? And what the hell is a foreign spy doing with a prospecting party on the shores of Great Bear Lake? Answer me that and I'll be almost satisfied!'

Her eyes dropped before his penetrating stare. 'I can't answer your questions,' she whispered tightly. 'Don't ask me any more . . . please.'

Brandon snorted. Just as he was getting to the root of the business, he thought savagely. Patience was the watchword, apparently. He thought: *You fool!* 'I suppose you won't tell me on account of this precious fellow Shawn?' he snapped. 'I'm disappointed in you.'

'I knew you would be.' There was just a trace of defiance in her tone. 'But, Rex, it's impossible.'

Brandon shrugged. 'Have it your own way,' he said in a tone of resignation. 'I still think you'd be wise to be frank with me. However . . . ' He rose to his feet, looking down at her with the beginnings of a smile on his lips. 'I'll go and see what I can knock up in the way of food. You'd better keep this while I'm out.' He undid his furs and gave her the revolver. 'Just in case,' he added.

She accepted the heavy weapon gravely. 'You do trust me, don't you?' she said enigmatically.

'I haven't much choice,' he answered a little flatly. 'So long for now, Steve. And stay in here.'

'I will,' she promised. 'Good luck.'

He went out, bending his head at the cave mouth and ducking through the opening. His luck was in. Less than half an hour later he was on his way back with a bag of one snow martin and a squirrel. Not a lot, he thought, but something to go on with.

He was five hundred yards from the cave when a dog barked.

The sound made him halt abruptly, listening and peering through the trees that screened his view. Nothing stirred, but again came a yapping bark that carried clearly in the thin, cold air. 'Company!' he muttered with quickened interest.

He started forward more cautiously, not knowing what the bark of the dog might mean. When he had covered another hundred yards, he heard a man's voice. It was curt and hard, and it followed closely on the heels of more barking. The barking stopped, to be replaced by the quieter yapping of more than one dog.

Brandon came within sight of the rocky vicinity of the cave. He stopped again, staring at the scene with mingled feelings. A full team of snow dogs and a sled were halted in front of the cave. Stephanie, a small, fur-huddled figure, was standing in the open near the fire, talking earnestly to a tall man whose back was to Brandon.

'Maybe lucky, maybe not,' muttered Brandon aloud. He made for the cave. Stephanie, he saw, did not have the gun in her hand. She caught sight of him and waved excitedly. The man with her swung round. He was clean-shaven, long faced, and very tall beside Stephanie.

'Rex!' she shouted. 'Come quickly! We're saved. Isn't it marvellous?'

Brandon said nothing in reply. He was

trying to make up his mind who this tall stranger might be. Out here in the wilds of the sub-arctic wastes, every man was suspect. Maybe Stephanie was a shade too gullible.

But when he drew close enough to see the man's face clearly, he felt an instant and definite liking for the fellow. There was something clean-cut and straight about the features that gave immediate confidence in their owner.

The man stared unsmilingly at Brandon. Brandon returned his scrutiny in like manner. Neither spoke for a moment. They were like a pair of strange dogs sizing each other up, not yet sure whether to fight or sniff noses. And Stephanie stood between them, looking first at Rex and then at the stranger.

Brandon was satisfied. 'I don't know who you are,' he said with a faint smile, 'but you're just in time for a meal.' He brought out the snow martin and tree rat, holding them up for inspection.

The man relaxed and grinned easily. 'That's welcome news,' he said. His voice was deep and firm. 'The lady was telling me something of how you're fixed. Was bad luck losing your team on the river. I guess you must be strangers to these parts, or you'd have known it was due for a break-up.'

Brandon hid a smile. Probing already! In these parts, a stranger was suspect. Yes, he'd thought the same about this man. It was only reasonable. 'We're new here,' he admitted. 'But it's quite a long story. Come in and make yourself at home. You're the most welcome person I can think of at the moment.'

The man — he was still in his twenties, decided Brandon — turned and walked between them to the cave. His dog team was a fine outfit; the huskies, lying quietly in the snow, following their master with liquid, amber eyes.

Stephanie busied herself building up the fire and preparing food, begging a pan from the stranger. When he brought it back from his sled, he brought food from his own supplies to swell the feast. The sled was remarkably well-stocked.

While they were waiting, the stranger freed his dogs and fed them with dried meat. Then he sat himself down in the mouth of the cave and watched Stephanie with curious intentness.

Brandon caught his eye. The man gave a cough and shifted his gaze. 'Care to tell me how you two come to be crossing this sector?' he enquired a moment later.

Brandon stretched himself comfortably against the rock of the cave, lighting his pipe with care. 'We're heading for Great Bear Lake,' he said slowly. 'You wouldn't be going in that direction, I suppose?'

The man neither admitted nor denied it. Brandon took the hint and plunged into their story, leaving out only those passages which directly affected Stephanie. Nor did he make any mention of Nicolas Shawn, still a shadowy entity somewhere in the background.

'You have quite a nerve to undertake a trip like this,' was the man's considered comment. 'Great Bear, eh? That's where I've come from, friend.' He grinned. 'But I'm sorry to hear about Jake.'

Brandon raised his eyebrows. 'You knew him, then?'

The man gave a nod. 'Many's the yarn

we've had when I've crossed his trap-lines and bedded in one of his shacks. Mighty fine feller, Jake.'

Brandon nodded thoughtfully. 'You're a trapper, too, I suppose ... ?' he said slowly.

'I collect a few pelts,' he admitted. 'So poor old Jake is dead an' buried, eh? Too bad ... And you came on here after taking his dogs. Mister, that could be kind of suspicious.' There was no trace of humour in his eyes.

Brandon's gaze was cold as he measured the man. 'I wouldn't say that if I were you,' he said softly. 'Not a healthy attitude to take, if you don't mind my saying so.'

The stranger shrugged almost carelessly. 'Forget it,' he said. 'I have a right to speak my mind. You're a queer pair to find in these parts, don't forget.'

Brandon sensed a danger to which he could not put a name. 'Are we?' he said.

The man gave a curt little nod.

'What are you going to do about it?' Brandon's tone was mild.

'Nothing ... yet. What's the big

attraction at Great Bear Lake?'

Stephanie, bending over the fire, turned her head to meet a quizzical stare from the stranger. 'What business is it of yours?' she said suddenly.

He smiled thinly. 'Maybe it isn't,' he said. 'I was only thinking of Jake being dead.'

There was tension creeping in among them now. Brandon said: 'If you think we killed him for his dogs, you're wrong. What were *you* doing at Great Bear, anyway?'

The man looked up, amused apparently. 'Passing through,' he replied. 'Tell me your reasons for going to Great Bear, and maybe I'll take you.'

Brandon told him about the prospecting party. He had to include Stephanie as a member of it too, but she raised no objection to the lie.

The stranger seemed satisfied. He nodded several times. 'I guess you'll pass,' he said, looking at Brandon. 'Never forget, mister, that when you're a long way from law and order, it doesn't pay to take things for what they seem at first.'

'I've already discovered that, thanks. While we're at it, who are you?'

The man smiled in a near-friendly fashion. 'Brown,' he answered. 'Just plain Brown.'

Brandon glanced at Stephanie. 'That's almost as common a name as Smith.' He wondered who Brown might be.

Stephanie shrugged. 'Yes, isn't it?' she murmured.

'Supper's ready. You'll join us, of course, Mr. Brown?'

Brown got to his feet. 'Try and stop me!' he said. 'I've been watching you cook, ma'am. You're quite a hand at it, if you'll pardon the liberty.'

Outwardly, at any rate, friendly relations had now been established. But Brandon was none too easy in his mind. Why was Brown so inordinately curious about them? Because of Jake being dead? Was that the only reason? A prickle of foreboding coursed up and down his spine as he took the food that Stephanie passed him.

8

Nicolas Shawn

It was a meal that Brandon remembered on many later occasions. Despite the superficial amity of the party, it was obvious that an undercurrent of mutual suspicion was still running swiftly through the minds of Brown on one side, and Brandon and Stephanie on the other. But above and beyond all that, there was always the unanswerable query regarding Nicolas Shawn. It burrowed like a weevil in Brandon's mind, and he was more troubled than he cared to admit as to what part Shawn was destined to play in Stephanie's life. That Shawn did have his place in the pattern he was certain. He wished she had been more frank, instead of hedging; but now that Brown had turned up, it seemed unlikely that she would loosen her tongue again. Whatever she might have told him would not be told in the presence of a third party.

Brown, on his part — just plain Brown — rarely took his eyes from her. To Brandon it seemed that the man was attempting to read her mind; to worm from it secrets that perhaps she herself barely recognised. And she, for reasons of her own, went out of her way to be friendly towards the enigmatic Brown. Acting as hostess, she positively sparkled, hiding whatever feelings of unease she might have behind a façade of gay and pleasant chatter.

It was not until the meal was almost ended that Brown turned to Brandon with a disarming smile. 'I guess I'll have to take you two where you're going,' he said. 'Too bad to leave a woman as nice as Miss Olsbert in the wilds to fend for herself!' He shook his head. 'No, sir, I couldn't do that.'

Stephanie beamed at him. 'Of course you'll take us to Great Bear,' she said. 'You couldn't refuse, could you?'

'I could; but I won't!'

Brandon shot a glance from one to the other of them. He had an uncomfortable feeling that Stephanie's friendliness was not entirely forced. There was a certain gleam in her eye that he had seen in the eyes of other women. For one awful moment he toyed with the idea that this man, this unknown Brown, might be a person connected in some mysterious way with Nicolas Shawn. He tried to thrust the ugly notion from his mind. Yet suppose Shawn had a rendezvous with a stranger in these parts? It was not such a mad idea. What was Brown doing trekking west from Great Bear Lake? To meet Shawn coming east? But Stephanie had hinted that Shawn was not mixed up in any trouble. And if Stephanie and Brown were known to each other already, they were making a wonderful job of not showing it. Brandon swore mentally and gave it up, defeated.

Brown said: 'I guess you're ready to start right away?'

Brandon brought his mind back to earth. 'We're very grateful to you,' he said guardedly.

The smile left Brown's lips for a fraction of a second. 'Save it,' he murmured briefly. 'Count yourselves lucky to be alive and let it go at that.'

The dog team was hitched and the sled repacked to make room for Stephanie. Brown personally saw to it that she was well wrapped up against the biting cold. Then he grinned at Brandon. 'Let's go,' he said, lifting his whip to crack it in the air. But before he could flex his wrist, there was a single sharp report: the *spang* of a rifle, crisp and clear, from not very far away.

Brandon gestured north. 'Somewhere over there!' he snapped. 'Come on!'

The shot was not repeated. The two men broke into a run, leaving Stephanie on the sled, a half-uttered protest on her lips.

Breaking through the fringe of a thicket of spruce, they stopped in their tracks. In the centre of a clear patch of snow stood a stationary dog team. Even from where they were, they could see that the sled had a broken runner and was heeled at an angle. But it was not the sled and its team that riveted their attention.

A few yards from where the sled had

stopped, a man lay on his side in the snow. His rifle was a black streak well out of reach of his hand. And a big bull moose was pawing the ground less than ten yards from the fallen man, who stared at it in fascinated horror. The great broad antlers were down as the beast gave an angry bawl and prepared to charge. Brandon had never seen such a perfectly presented shot. The moose was standing broadside on, its heart exposed; and the range was negligible.

The double report of their rifles merged into one. Just as the moose started forward for the prostrate man, it was hit and felled as if a battering-ram had struck it in the side, never to move again from the spot where it lay.

Without a word, they ran towards the fallen man. He was getting up stiffly, retrieving his rifle and coming to meet them. 'And I guess I thought miracles didn't happen!' he said. His accent was American, and the moment Brandon saw his face he knew that Nicolas Shawn was no longer a bodiless name.

Through the turmoil in his mind, he

heard Brown saying something to Shawn. What would happen now? He was watching Brown like a hawk. Did they know each other? But Brown's expression showed nothing more sinister than genuine concern and sympathy.

Brandon looked hard at Shawn. The man had not changed much in facial appearance since the time of the snapshot in Stephanie's wallet. His clothes were different, naturally, and there was a fair stubble of beard on his chin, but the features were unmistakable.

Brown grinned and glanced at the slaughtered moose. 'Lucky we happened along,' he said. 'Did he sneak up on you?'

Shawn gestured to the sled. 'I was fixing a runner,' he explained. 'It came at me when my back was turned, and I only had time for one shot. Missed, of course. When I tried to run for cover in the trees over there, it knocked me flying. I guess I thought that was the end!' He gave a rueful grin. 'Then you folks turned up. 'Don't know what I can say to thank you, but I reckon you'll understand.'

Brown waved it aside with an airy

gesture. 'You'd best come and join us,' he suggested. His grey eyes were fixed on Shawn as he spoke.

Shawn said thanks, that was fine. He called his dogs together and started the broken sled moving slowly. He was limping a little as he walked.

Brandon looked at the dead moose. There were two bullet holes in its side a few inches behind the shoulder. Less than half an inch separated the wounds from each other.

They took the damaged sled through the trees to where Stephanie was waiting, or had been waiting. She came to meet them when they were halfway back. Brandon literally held his breath. Stephanie came to a halt when she caught sight of them. Maybe the unexpected shock of seeing Nicolas Shawn had robbed her of movement; Brandon did not know. He tried to read her expression, but she was too far away. He tried watching Shawn for signs of recognition. There were none. Then they were close enough for Brandon to see both their faces clearly.

Incredibly enough, it was only Stephanie who showed emotion that might have been something other than normal curiosity and casual interest. Her face had a slightly stiff, rather frozen look for a second or two. Brandon glanced swiftly at Shawn. The man's expression was a mingling of pleasant surprise, interest in a pretty woman, and curiosity as to why she was there. By the time Brandon looked back at Stephanie, she was smiling, in complete control of her feelings again.

Brown nodded slowly, as if to himself. His features were blank, eyes veiled. Then he grinned with a swift return to pleasant good humour. 'We're adding to the party, Miss Olsbert,' he said clearly.

Stephanie smiled at Shawn. Her politeness left nothing to be desired. But Brandon, watching Shawn unobtrusively, saw a sudden shadow cross his face — a baffled, puzzled expression, thought Brandon, troubled in mind. The name of Olsbert meant something to Shawn. But what?

Stephanie murmured an acknowledgement of Brown's remark.

Shawn stepped forward, smiling and glancing enquiringly at Brown, whom he seemed to accept as leader of the party. 'My name's Harris,' he said. 'And you . . . ?'

Brown introduced himself and Brandon. Brandon was too confused in his thoughts to do more than nod. So Shawn was Harris, was he? But this was definitely Shawn, which meant that Harris was a phoney name — just as Smith had been. And, perhaps, Brown . . . Brandon did not like it. He did not like it at all, any of it.

Stephanie was saying: 'Well, now that you've joined us, Mr. Harris, we'd better hold up proceedings and make some more coffee!' Her voice was light, friendly. They were back at the mouth of the cave by this time. The fire was quickly rebuilt and stoked; coffee set to warm. In the meantime, Brown was going to work on the broken runner of Shawn's sled. Shawn himself — or Harris — was watching him, dividing his attention between the task in hand and Stephanie.

Brown came back, announcing that the

sled was as good as new. He bent his gaze on Shawn. 'Where were you bound for?' he enquired in a casual tone.

Shawn's answer came with only the fraction of a second's hesitation. 'Somewhere in the Great Bear district,' he said.

Brown considered in silence for a space. Brandon felt his heart beginning to thump. He glanced at Stephanie, but she was busy with the coffee pot, head bent.

'Mightily popular place this time of year,' mused Brown.

Shawn gave a shrug. 'I wouldn't know,' he answered.

'We're all going that way,' said Brown. 'Where do you come from, friend?' His head was inclined a little to one side, watchful.

Shawn eyed him with barely veiled animosity. 'West of here,' he said flatly. 'You're a pretty inquisitive man, aren't you?'

Brown was suddenly smiling again. 'I guess you get that way living all alone in this kind of country.'

Shawn grunted. Then: 'Do you have any food to spare for my dogs?' he asked, changing a subject that might or might not be dangerous.

Brown strode across to his own sled, unlashing the cover at the front. Shawn went with him, close on his heels. Brandon and Stephanie, together on the other side of the fire, watched narrowly.

When Brandon spoke, it was in little more than a whisper: 'You know who that is as well as I do, Steve. Shawn! What's it all about? Doesn't he know you? He recognised your name all right.'

But Stephanie only smiled in a give-nothing fashion, her eyes still fixed on the other two men. 'He's rather sweet, isn't he?' she murmured. 'Brown, I mean . . .'

Brandon hid his irritation. 'You wait a while!' he said curtly. 'There's trouble brewing if I'm not mistaken.'

She looked up at him, small nose wrinkled in a teasing smile. 'Jealous?' she breathed.

Brandon snorted, angry in spite of his liking for her. Damn it, he thought, what did it matter if he was jealous? He wasn't, anyway!

Brown and Shawn were feeding the latter's dogs. They did not appear to be talking while they worked.

'With any luck we can get rid of Brown,' murmured Brandon, forgetting his annoyance with Stephanie.

'You'll do nothing of the kind!' she said quickly.

'Why not?'

'Because I like him, for one thing. And besides — '

'He's mixed up in the same thing you are!' Brandon completed what he thought was in her mind.

She laughed softly. 'Rex, you're impossible! Why do you jump to such absurd conclusions all the time? I've never seen him in my life before.'

'Or Shawn either, I suppose?' said Brandon acidly.

She swung on him at that, her brown eyes no longer amused. 'Or Shawn either!' she whispered fiercely.

'He knew your name.' Brandon's voice was stubborn.

'Of course. I'll tell you why later . . . maybe.'

'Ah! So there *is* a connection . . . ?'

'Be quiet, will you? They're coming back!'

Shawn grinned at Stephanie. Brown treated her to a smile. Brandon still couldn't decide whether he liked the man or not. He looked all right, but that was as far as he felt like going.

'All fixed, Miss Olsbert,' said Brown. 'We can move when you like now.'

'If Harris is making for Great Bear Lake, there won't be any need for you to go back,' said Brandon. 'It's good of you to offer, naturally, but we should hate to put you out.' He could almost feel the annoyance in Stephanie's eyes as they rested on him briefly.

Brown smiled and shook his head. 'This is wolf country,' he said. 'As a native of the place, it's my special responsibility to see you all safe. And besides — ' He gestured to Shawn. ' — Mr. Harris's sled isn't all that strong even now. I'll tag along if I may.'

Stephanie's smile was ravishing. 'We're delighted to have you,' she murmured. 'Rex was only trying to be helpful.' She shot a look at Brandon that was sugar and vinegar mixed.

Brown inclined his head gravely. 'Shall we go then?' he said. 'I'll travel with Harris if you've no objection.'

Stephanie had none. Brandon kept his own to himself. Shawn seemed to accept the position with a readiness that puzzled him.

Brown said: 'Now remember, this is wolf country, folks. Keep together if you know what's good, and when I say keep together I mean it.' He looked at them all in turn, his grey eyes missing nothing.

The whips cracked loudly. They were on the move, with Brandon and Stephanie bringing up the rear. It was a new experience to Brandon to be relegated to a back seat. He decided to change things around before long, but first he must discover more of what was going on in Stephanie's complex mind. He realised now that there were moments in his desperate efforts to make her talk when he had acted like a spoilt child. He regretted them, but they did not deter him from trying again.

Brown set a fast pace, but never more than a few seconds elapsed before he glanced over his shoulder to see that they were following. There was a distance of fifty or sixty yards between them.

Stephanie was silent. Brandon had to speak to her twice before she answered. 'Steve!' he said suddenly, almost in her ear.

She looked up at him from the sled. 'Don't shout,' she said. 'I'm not deaf.'

'Do you realise the position we're in?' he went on grimly. 'Your friend Brown has no intention of parting from us. Or from Shawn. He's probably Shawn's confederate anyway. We couldn't get away at the moment if we tried — not without a fight.'

Her answer surprised him. 'I know that. It worries me a little. I realised it just before we started. What do you think I feel like, Rex?' She turned her head and stared at him. There was a desperate, panicky light in her eyes that was alien to them.

'Rather like sitting on a volcano, isn't it?' he said. 'I thought you knew Shawn?

Why didn't he acknowledge you?'

She sighed. 'It was your idea that we knew each other,' she pointed out. '*I* never said so!'

Brandon's jaw tightened in exasperation. 'Steve, why won't you tell me what's going on?'

'You searched my wallet, didn't you?' she countered. 'In it you found a photograph and a news clipping. Nicolas Shawn — if you really want to know — is engaged to my sister, Ingrid. She doesn't know I have that snapshot, but I had to have something to tell me when I met him. I've never seen him before, and under the circumstances I couldn't very well introduce myself as his future sister-in-law, could I? Of course, the name Olsbert rang a bell in his mind, but I don't think he guessed who I was.'

'Now we're getting somewhere! But you do know why Shawn is making for Great Bear, don't you? If you didn't, you wouldn't be so worried.' He paused, giving her time, but she still refused to talk. Brandon continued: 'Shawn's up to no good. It's my belief that the foreign agent who's managed to sneak in on Vetjek's party is due to take over secrets from him.' His tone was bitter. 'My God, Steve, it's a dirty game! I must say I'm surprised at your being mixed up in it.'

'You've got it all wrong, as usual,' she told him flatly. 'Ingrid was sent to Great Bear under cover of her geological qualifications for the express purpose of contacting Nick.'

Brandon frowned. 'But why? Why does Shawn have to light out suspiciously in order to contact another American operative somewhere in the Canadian wilds? It just doesn't make any sense!'

'But it does. It does if you weren't so pig-headed as to keep on thinking of Nick as a melodramatic villain-of-the-piece.'

'What do you mean by that?'

'Simply, Rex, that the reason for his rendezvous with Ingrid is not to pass on information of the kind you imagine, but to tell her something of an entirely different nature. Information, in fact, that he himself has gleaned from America's potential enemies! Now do you understand?'

146

Brandon frowned as he steered the sled over the snow. Things were taking shape in his mind, but there were still a great many gaps to be filled.

'Then why the hue and cry?' he said presently. 'And why does Shawn have to trek across country like a fugitive if he's working in the interests of his own government?'

'You're good at asking questions, aren't you?'

'Better than you are at answering them! Have I run up against another wall?'

'No-o . . . Maybe it's because I trust you more than I did. Maybe it's because now that Brown is with us, the situation is altered slightly.'

'But the hue and cry?'

'It should never have started,' she said. 'It all began when some self-righteous public-spirited humbug found out about his leaving and spread the alarm. Before it could be blanketed and silenced, the news boys got hold of it, and of course it was misinterpreted. It was too late then to keep things quiet; a gagging move on the part of the U.S. government would have aroused suspicion in just the quarters we didn't want it roused in. It would have seemed fishy, you see?'

Brandon smiled faintly. 'More or less,' he admitted. 'It seems I've been wronging Shawn.' He paused. 'But how do you know all this, Steve? Where do *you* come in?' His eyes were curious as he studied her face for a moment.

'I'm an undercover operative myself,' she said. 'Not a very good one, perhaps, but that's my own fault.'

'Oh . . . Now I understand why you didn't like answering questions. You seem to be in this up to the neck. Sorry if I misjudged you in the first place. What about this alien in Vetjek's party? Does Shawn know about him?'

She shook her head, huddling the furs round her to keep out the cold. The short day was drawing to a close, and the icy quality of the air was intensified. 'He doesn't know,' she said. 'What I aimed to do was get to Great Bear and warn Ingrid, leaving her to put Shawn on his guard.'

'I see. But why pick on Great Bear,

Steve? That's what I can't follow.'

She sighed. 'As far as I can tell you, the reason is that Shawn's information has to do directly with Vetjek's prospecting activities. I'm told that the outcome of this expedition may be vital to the western powers. Don't ask me how.'

Brandon frowned. There appeared to be considerably more to his invitation to join Hans Vetjek than he had realised. He wished people were more explicit. Gold was valuable, but the safety of the western world did not depend on it. He had been given to understand that Vetjek was hoping to find gold in large quantities on a mountain called Ectal Borrn, above Great Bear Lake.

'It ties up all right,' he mused. 'Your sister, Ingrid, was put in the party to watch American interests. Shawn has something to pass on, personally it seems, and was directed to contact his own fiancée on the spot. Unknown to both of them, an alien agent is also there — presumably to sneak around on behalf of his own country. Your department knows that and sends you out on the job.

Couldn't they have warned Vetjek by radio instead of going to all that trouble?'

She shook her head. 'The risk of putting the enemy on his guard would have been too great,' she contended. 'It's better this way, Rex. The personal touch, you know.'

Brandon sniffed doubtfully. It was growing colder. 'It's Brown who worries me,' he said slowly. 'I can't size him up at all.'

'Leave it be. There's no need to do a thing unless he definitely turns against us, which I don't think he will. He's taking us to Great Bear Lake. What more could we wish for?'

Brandon considered. There was something in what she said. But he still did not like it. 'All right,' he said. 'Will you make yourself known to Shawn if you get the chance?'

'Perhaps. I'm not sure yet.'

Darkness was falling. Brown called a halt for the night. The fire was lit and food prepared. Brown was more silent and taciturn than of late. There was something on his mind. Brandon caught him watching Shawn, frowning as he did so. He barely spoke a word till the meal was ended, then he looked across at Shawn in the leaping firelight.

'I've a hunch you're a fugitive from justice, Harris,' he announced. 'The name should be Nicolas Shawn.' His hand moved swiftly. 'No, don't try that! I've got you covered, Shawn!'

9

'Tomorrow . . . '

Nicolas Shawn was a stiff, dark shadow on the other side of the fire. His right hand had started to move towards his hip, but was now still, halfway to the gun he carried.

For a moment no one spoke. Then it was Stephanie who broke the silence. 'What is this?' she said in a frightened whisper. 'Brown, are you crazy?'

Brown took his eyes from Shawn for just an instant. 'No, ma'am,' he said. 'This is — ' But he got no further. Shawn moved as if a powerful spring had been released underneath him. One second he was crouching on the snow; the next he was up and flinging himself towards the cover of the trees a yard or two away.

Brown's gun came up, stiffened, fired. But the light was impossible. Then, before he could fire again, Brandon acted. His broad body catapulted clean across Stephanie as she gave a little cry of dismay. Outstretched arms closed over Brown's lean hips. The two men went down together, rolling and panting in the powdery snow. Brown's gun went off again, ploughing a gash in Brandon's fur coat. The man was fighting mad now. Brandon got a grip on his wrist and started bending it backwards. The revolver dropped from Brown's fingers and lay on the snow. Then Brown succeeded in twisting round, forcing Brandon over, getting astride him. His teeth were bared savagely as he grunted and struggled for mastery.

Brandon felt his senses swimming. From the corner of his eye he saw Brown stretch out to pick up the revolver. Then Stephanie took a hand. There was a crunch of footsteps in the snow, and the butt of a rifle landed hard on the back of Brown's fur-capped head. His weight was suddenly dead on top of Brandon. Stephanie dropped the rifle and dragged at Brown. Brandon wriggled out from underneath him, still breathing hard.

'Shawn!' he panted. 'The fool's got away!'

Stephanie looked at him fearfully. 'I've killed him!' she whispered. 'Rex, I've killed him! Oh . . . '

Brandon gripped her shoulder. 'Steady!' he snapped. She dropped to her knees beside the body of Brown, hurriedly searching for the life beat she had feared was gone. When she found it, there was more relief in her eyes than Brandon had ever seen before.

'He's all right,' she breathed. Her eyes closed tightly for a moment.

'Pity,' said Brandon heartlessly. 'He was ready to kill me for interfering. We'd better tie him up and find Shawn before he's lost.' He glanced down at Brown. There was a puzzled frown on his forehead as he fetched a length of cord from one of the sleds. How in the world, he asked himself, had Brown known Shawn for the man he was? All his previous ideas about Brown were disrupted. He could not be a friend of Shawn's; instead he was an enemy.

He tied Brown securely, looking round

for Stephanie to see where she was, but there was no sign of her. Brandon muttered a curse and started running over the tracks left by Shawn. In places it was possible to see they were doubled. Stephanie had followed Shawn ahead of him. He came on them unexpectedly, abruptly. Shawn stood with his back to a tall, thick tree. His face was a white smudge. There was a gun in his hand and Stephanie was a yard away, her hands lifted slightly as she stared through the gloom.

Shawn saw Brandon coming. 'Keep out of this!' he said harshly. 'Both of you, understand? I've got a job to do and no one's going to stop me. Stay back, Brandon!' He looked about cautiously, seeking Brown perhaps, expecting a sneak attack from another direction,

'Don't be a damned fool, Shawn,' said Brandon grimly. 'If you want the truth, Brown's back there by the fire, tied up. Stephanie's your future sister-in-law.' He appealed to her: 'Tell him, Steve. Make him see that he's wrong to try running out.'

Shawn said nothing; nor did Stephanie. Then Shawn came slowly from where he stood, still with his gun out, and a queer half-credulous look on his face. 'You're crazy!' he whispered. 'Who's Brown? What are you doing here?'

'Put that gun up and act as if you had a brain,' countered Brandon. 'Steve will tell you all about it. Come back to the fire — this is no place to talk.'

Shawn looked at Stephanie, bending forward to see her clearly in the darkness. 'Is this on the level?' he asked.

She nodded wordlessly. 'It's vital that you get on to Great Bear,' she added. 'Ingrid's in danger. Who Brown is, I don't know, but we've dealt with him.'

Shawn was satisfied. 'Ingrid . . . ' he whispered. 'Come on, both of you!' He started walking rapidly through the trees, kicking up snow as he went. And Stephanie was talking now, talking fast, telling him all she knew and appealing to Brandon for confirmation.

When they reached the little camp, they found Brown awake, glaring at them in the light of the flames with all the malice of a beaten man who will never recognise defeat. They regarded him curiously.

'So you're all in it, eh?' snapped Brown. His voice was slurred from the ache in his head. 'I guess you don't know what you're running your necks into!'

Brandon stood over him. 'What we did we had to do,' he said. 'Our work is of national and international importance. We can't afford to let a stranger meddle and put us out of gear. Now it's your turn to answer a question or two.'

Brown actually smiled, and glanced at Stephanie. But he said nothing, waiting for Brandon.

'How did you know this man was Nicolas Shawn?' Brandon asked. There was more curiosity in his tone than any other emotion. He was not exactly angry with Brown when he came to think about it.

Brown gave another faint smile. Then: 'So he *is* Shawn? Well, that's something at any rate. I wasn't absolutely sure.'

'That won't help you much,' put in Shawn. 'Who the hell are you?'

Brown eyed him shrewdly for an

instant. 'Sergeant Brown of the North-west Mounted Police,' he said grimly. 'If you people can think up a yarn to satisfy me, you'll be just about the cleverest lot in the world.'

Brandon swore afterwards that his mind stopped working completely for seconds on end.

Stephanie put a hand to her mouth and gave a little cry of dismay.

Shawn leant forward, muttering to himself. 'Oh Lord!' he said a moment later. 'That *has* torn it!'

Brandon took a grip on himself. That Brown might be a Mountie had never entered his head. Somehow he had forgotten every sentence about the law in these isolated parts of the world. But he knew the motto of the Mounties; and he knew, too, that to Brown they must all show up in the worst possible light — especially after attacking him in the course of his duty. Whichever way he looked at the problem, it was ugly. The only chance they stood of righting the situation was to make Brown believe that Shawn was not what he appeared to be. He turned to Stephanie.

'You'd better do the talking,' he said. 'It's your show, really. Yours and Shawn's. And make it good, Steve. There are two alternatives, remember. One is that Brown is made to see the light; the other that we take him with us as a prisoner, the final result of which will be lengthy and unpleasant for all of us.'

Stephanie glanced apprehensively at Brown, who stared back at her, giving nothing away. Shawn lit a cigarette with slow and elaborate care.

It was Stephanie who began the story; Shawn who took it up and completed it with his own share. Brandon added all he himself knew. And when the telling was done, they watched Sergeant Brown anxiously. Far better, if possible, to have the man working with them than against them.

'You know,' said Brown slowly, 'by all the rules, I should arrest the lot of you and take you straight to my base H.Q.'

'But you won't, Sergeant, will you?' begged Stephanie. 'You're just the man we'll need when we get to Great Bear

Lake. You'll have duty enough then. Please!'

Brown grinned. 'I admire guts. But there are several technical difficulties. By rights I should take you to base, as I said. If I go along to Great Bear, I'm risking a lot — my job and all that. But I'll take the chance on one condition.'

'And that is?'

'That you surrender to me unconditionally, handing over your weapons and travelling under arrest. I'm prepared, however, to accept your paroles, so that the state will only be a technical one. All I demand is your armoury, which is only fair.'

Stephanie looked at her companions. Her eyes were bright with relief. 'I'm quite prepared to do as he asks,' she said. 'When we find that spy at Great Bear, he'll be bound to withdraw the charges against us. We'll have proved ourselves innocent people.'

Brandon nodded and smiled. The situation had its humour, he thought. Here was Sergeant Brown, still trussed up securely, arresting them and accepting their parole in the same breath.

'Shawn . . . ?' he said. 'How about it?'

'Suits me,' the man agreed. 'Hadn't we better free our friend now? After all,' he added with a grin, 'he *is* arresting us.'

Brown was untied hurriedly. Now that the matter was settled, more or less, he gave no signs of bearing malice for the treatment he had received. In fact, somewhat to the surprise of everyone, he congratulated Stephanie on the way she had knocked him out.

'My mistake for not counting a woman dangerous!' he added good-humouredly. 'I'll remember another time!'

There was more talk. Brown admitted that he had been suspicious of Shawn's identity from the very first, but had only been able to check against a detailed description of the missing man when they stopped for the night. For various reasons of his own, he had not explained previously that he was a policeman. Had he done so, things might have worked out differently.

The only thing that now worried Stephanie was whether the arrival of so many people at Great Bear would put the unknown foreign agent on his guard.

'I think it ought to sort itself out,' said Shawn. 'And in any case, Steve, we'll keep our eyes open. The odds are that he'll give himself away.'

'Isn't there anyone we can trust besides Ingrid in the party?' queried Stephanie gravely.

'I've known Hans Vetjek for something like fifteen years,' put in Brandon. 'He may be able to give us a line to work on.' He glanced at Shawn. 'Wouldn't it be wise if you shared this secret information of yours with a third person?' he suggested. 'Suppose something happened to you? No one here could carry on with your work.'

Shawn took no offence. He admitted that it would be a shame if anything did happen to him, but at the same time was not prepared to divulge his information to anyone else — even his future sister-in-law.

'You see, folks,' he drawled, 'it's so big I'd be scared to trust even my own mother. Till I get to Great Bear and contact Ingrid, I just can't talk. Afterwards it won't make all that much difference. All I can say is that my mission concerns the ground over which Vetjek's prospecting outfit plans to work this spring. You'll have to be satisfied with that.'

They were forced to accept it; but during the days that followed, the scientist's refusal to talk in no way hindered the growing friendship that was spreading through the party. Stephanie and Brown spent a great deal of time together, and it did not require a seer to guess what was happening to them. Shawn and Brandon found a lot in common.

On the last night they were less than a half day's march from Great Bear Lake. Snow, wolves and cold were the common enemies of sleep, but their spirits were high. They camped in the lee of a pine thicket, the dancing light of the fire reflected on their faces.

'Tomorrow,' said Brown definitely. 'Tomorrow's the day, folks!'

Shawn nodded. 'Yes,' he mused soberly. 'Tomorrow . . .'

10

The Man Who Ran

Brown raised his arm and pointed wordlessly. The cold blue surface of Great Bear Lake was visible a mile away. Wind off the mountains ruffled the water. There was thick ice close in shore, but further out it was broken and floating. A definite break in the shore ice showed where the outfall of the Mackenzie came in. Trees grew down almost to the water's edge along most of the shore within their range of vision.

'There it is,' said Brown. 'Great Bear Lake. We should make our final plans before going any further.'

They nodded, talking things over, making decisions. When they started again, Stephanie was travelling with Brandon. 'Do you know where Vetjek is camped?' she asked.

Brandon pointed with his arm, indicating a large humpbacked hill rising two or three miles to the north. 'That's Ectal Borrn,' he said. 'I've checked on the map and confirmed it from Vetjek's description. The cabin they're using as a base camp is close to the lake at the foot of the mountain.'

She was satisfied.

'How are you getting on with Brown?' he asked presently.

She flushed a little. 'He's awfully nice when you get to know him well,' she murmured. 'I like him a lot.'

Brandon smiled. 'I've met a lot worse,' he said. Then his eyes narrowed as he sighted movement in the distance. The smoke of a fire rose slantwise from a stone chimney on the far side of a shallow crest.

'I think we're almost there,' he said quietly, turning to make a sign to Brown in the rear. 'Keep your fingers crossed, Steve!'

Ten minutes later, the two sleds were skimming down a final slope to come to rest in front of a long, low log-built cabin. Their arrival was heralded by the barking of dogs, and a moment later the door of the cabin opened to reveal the figure of Hans Vetjek himself. He stood watching curiously, not recognising Brandon at once. Then a broad smile spread over his face as he hurried forward.

Vetjek was short and broad, with powerful shoulders and a pleasantly ugly face that bore a sabre scar on one cheek. It gave him a slightly sinister appearance till he smiled, then his dark eyes were transformed, and the whole of his features conspired to give an immediate impression of warmth and good humour.

Brandon strode forward to meet him, hand outstretched. 'I made it at last, Hans,' he said. 'Sorry to be late, but there was trouble on the way.' He gave a brief résumé of the plane wreck, then gestured to Stephanie and the others. 'These people joined me en route,' he explained. 'There's an injured man on the second sled; and I think this young lady is the sister of one of your party.'

Vetjek went across to where Brown's team stood panting. His eyes were full of concern as he peered at the 'injured' man. Nicolas Shawn wore so many bandages round his face and head that only his nose and one eye were visible. Brandon said something vague about a tree having fallen on him. He did not know who the man was, he added. There was nothing on him to say, and since finding him after meeting Brown he had not been able to tell them anything.

Vetjek took it all in without a murmur, accepting the arrival of four people instead of only one with good grace. 'I am alone on the site at the moment,' he said. 'The others have gone out on a preliminary survey, but will be back before nightfall. You must make yourself at home.' He beamed at Stephanie. 'I did not even know that Ingrid had a sister,' he said, 'let alone such a charming one.' He bowed very slightly as he said it.

Shawn was carried carefully into the cabin and put to bed, while Vetjek bustled round like a mother hen, preparing a meal for which the newcomers were ready enough — all save Shawn, who gave a few realistic groans. Brown made a pretence of tending him with the utmost care.

'Wait till Ingrid comes back,' said

Vetjek. 'She'll look after him. She's a better doctor than any of us here.'

Brandon seized the opening. 'Hans,' he began, 'before the others arrive, I should like to know something about them. Remember that I only know their names.'

Vetjek grinned and wagged his head. 'Always ready for adventure, Rex,' he said. 'I knew you'd come whatever I suggested. Well, now, there are four other men and Ingrid.' He lifted his hand, ticking them off one by one on his fingers as he talked. 'There's Grants. He's an explosive expert. No better in the world to my knowledge. Then we have Tony Bayne, another Englishman like yourself. His speciality is finding gold, which I hope will be rich in Ectal Borrn. Next comes Hiram Weston, from the States. He's a general geologist, and seems pretty capable, though I don't know him well. And the last man, besides myself, is Piet Lienzget, a naturalised Canadian. He's reputed to know all there is to be known about the handling of certain instruments we have in our equipment, and I hope they're right. Personally I don't care much for the fellow, but that may be nothing to go on. And last, but by no means least, of course, there's Ingrid. She's a Yank with a yen for sulphur.'

Brandon grinned. 'I'm surprised at you taking a woman along on a thing like this,' he said lightly.

'Washington wanted a finger in the pie for defence reasons, it seems. We didn't object, and we've never regretted her inclusion in the outfit. But you'll see for yourself when she turns up.'

Brandon said: 'Well, thanks for the catalogue. I'm interested to meet all these people.' He broke off and searched for words. Then: 'This is a pretty big thing. I suppose you're sure of all your party . . . ? I mean, what with all these scares running through the country . . . well, it might be a good thing for a potential enemy agent to keep an eye on developments up in these parts.' He watched the man closely. But Vetjek only blinked and stared at him. Then he laughed.

'Rex,' he said, 'this isn't worthy of you! You can take it as gospel that all this outfit is honest. They're a mixed bunch, I agree, but geology knows no boundaries.'

'That's just what I'm afraid of,' answered Brandon dryly. 'Anyhow, forget it, Hans. I'm probably an old woman!'

They laughed together. A moment later there was a shout from outside the cabin. Almost before Brandon could brace himself, the door burst open and three men and a woman came in. They halted abruptly at sight of the newcomers, then the woman gave a little cry of pleasure and ran towards Stephanie. The two women met and hugged each other, while Vetjek made a short introduction between Brandon, Brown and the other three.

They were Bayne, Grants and Weston. Piet Lientzget, Brandon learnt, was following on alone. No one seemed very keen about the man, and they were all too busy making their guests welcome to bother about him.

Nicolas Shawn, lying in a bunk at the far end of the cabin, caused a certain amount of concern, and Stephanie quickly took her sister across to see him. The men left them to it, but Brandon noticed that Ingrid was very quiet and had a strained look on her face when she returned with Stephanie. It was obvious that in re-dressing the 'injured' man, she had learnt his identity, though whether anything had passed between them or not he did not know. He caught a glance from Stephanie, but it told him nothing.

They all sat down round the big pine table, chatting and eating. Only Lientzget was absent. Brandon looked round, wondering which of these men was an enemy — Tony Bayne, the Englishman, a youngish, fair-haired giant with a ready laugh and a humorous mouth; or Grants, the dark and taciturn explosive expert with a strong American accent and a liking for chewing gum? Or Weston, a nondescript-looking little fellow with a cast in one eye and mousy-coloured hair going thin on top? Was he a foreign agent? Or was it the missing Lientzget, a man they none of them liked much; a man whose ability was an unknown quantity? Brandon could not answer his self-posed questions, but he meant to before many hours were out. And why, why, he asked himself again and again, had Nick Shawn made this journey? Only Shawn could tell them that, and Shawn was pretending injury and keeping his own counsel.

It was while Brandon was wracking his brain behind a façade of intelligent conversation with Vetjek and Bayne that Ingrid left the table and went quietly across to the bunk where Shawn lay silent and still. No one followed her, and Brandon knew that if the man was waiting an opportunity to tell her something this was his chance.

Piet Lientzget came in shaking snow from his furs and stamping his big feet a minute or two later. He glanced round and took off his top coat, hanging it behind the door without speaking. His face was unfriendly, and a cold glint showed in his eyes when he saw and was introduced to the newcomers.

'You make this place a travellers' rest, Hans,' he said sneeringly. 'A pity we've nothing better to do!'

They eyed him bleakly, Brandon, Brown and Stephanie. No wonder Lientzget's companions disliked him, thought Brandon.

The man turned his gaze on to Vetjek. 'I've some news for you,' he said. His voice was thick and a little slurred. Vetjek looked up mildly. 'Will it keep, Piet?' he said.

Lientzget shrugged. 'As you like,' he replied. His eyes came to rest on Brandon. 'Maybe it will be better to wait before talking in front of strangers.' He showed his teeth in a humourless grin, glancing at Stephanie and Brown as he did so. Then he pulled out a chair and sat down, eating greedily.

In the ensuing silence, which had an uncomfortable quality about it, Brandon heard Ingrid speaking quietly to Shawn in the far corner of the cabin. She came back to the table a moment afterwards, looking round at their faces with an uneasy smile. 'Can I have some soup for the invalid?' she said.

Vetjek hastened to spoon some into a dish and hand it to her. Lientzget said: 'How come he mussed his face?'

'Tree came down on him,' lied Brandon swiftly.

Lientzget went on eating noisily. The

rest of them left the table, scattering about the cabin or going outside to do various jobs before darkness fell. Only Lientzget remained at the table. He was still eating when Ingrid came back from the bunk and spoke quietly to Vetjek, who glanced at her sharply, then nodded his head. The two of them went outside together. Brandon rose to his feet from where he sat by the stove. His eyes met those of Stephanie for an instant, then he followed Vetjek out through the door.

Ingrid and Vetjek had paused outside, then moved on to another door at the far end of the cabin. Inside was a small radio room, with the mast and aerial standing stiffly from the ridge of the roof. Brandon followed them in before they realised he was behind them.

Vetjek turned swiftly, frowning. He relaxed when he saw it was Brandon, but Ingrid's mouth tightened up at the corners. Brandon said: 'Did you get Shawn's message all right?'

Ingrid drew a sharp breath, her hands clenched at her sides. 'You know about it?' she whispered. 'You know what it is?'

174

Brandon shook his head. 'No, but we've been working together. I learnt a lot from Steve on the way. What did Shawn have to tell you, Ingrid? You've got to tell us!'

She hesitated. 'There's someone here who is working against us,' she murmured. 'Steve told me that. She was sent up by Washington to warn me. Nick brought news of the greatest importance.' She turned to Vetjek. 'Hans,' she said, 'we aren't the first people to prospect Ectal Borrn. Nick has definite proof that a party of foreigners were here three years ago, secretly. He found out by accident during the course of his work in Alaska. But what's even more important, he obtained a map of results of their work on the mountain.'

'So that's why he made the trip personally . . . ?' mused Brandon. 'Yes, it makes sense now; but what about it?'

Ingrid dropped her voice even lower. 'There's gold in the hill,' she said quietly, 'but I've been ordered to prospect the northeastern shoulder for something else.'

'You, Ingrid?' Vetjek sounded puzzled.

'But your speciality is sulphur, isn't it?'

She nodded. 'Exactly! The section indicated is almost pure sulphur, and you know what a crying need there is for that in the world today. Think of it, Hans! A hill of the stuff.'

'But the other people know about it already?' said Brandon.

She nodded again. 'That's why I have to do it on my own. Nick has been told to put us on to the gold-bearing sector. Under cover of the natural excitement of finding gold, I can go ahead in the northeast.'

Vetjek shook his head in puzzlement. 'But, my dear,' he protested, 'why the secrecy if these foreigners already know about Ectal Borrn being sulphur-bearing?'

She bit her lower lip. 'There's one of them here in our midst,' she said tensely. 'Nick has discovered that if we show any interest in the northeast, we'll meet with all kinds of trouble. They don't mind us finding the gold, but sulphur is a different matter at the moment. Steps have been taken already to wipe us all out if the need arises. Don't ask me how, but that's what Nick says. He doesn't know himself.'

Brandon frowned. 'How on earth could any one man guarantee to destroy six people at a given time?' he said slowly. 'There's only night-time when you're all together . . . It could be done, though.' His eyes were troubled.

The other two were staring at him anxiously. 'You mean?' Ingrid whispered.

'I mean by blowing this cabin sky-high with dynamite!' said Brandon curtly. 'If charges are already set — and there isn't any reason why they shouldn't be — all our friend has to do is wait patiently for the right moment. If you show any signs of finding sulphur, all he's got to do is sneak outside the very next night and press the button. He doesn't know that we know Ectal Borrn has already been tested. It would merely be a regrettable accident, with only one survivor.'

Vetjek waved his hands unhappily. 'But such a callous thing,' he muttered. 'Who would do it, Rex?'

Brandon's jaw hardened. 'An explosives

expert, maybe. Didn't you say Grants was the local one?'

Vetjek waved it aside impatiently. 'I've known Jim Grants for forty years. We went to school together. No, Rex, not Grants. Definitely not him.'

'In this kind of business, you can't trust your best friend,' retorted Brandon. He turned to Ingrid. 'Whatever you do, don't breathe a word about sulphur to anyone. And avoid the northeast sector till we know our enemy!'

She nodded dumbly. Vetjek wore an unhappy expression, deeply troubled by the whole affair.

'What about Nick?' said Ingrid.

'No one must know who he is. You'd better make yourself his personal nurse, Ingrid. And I repeat: stay away from the northea — ' Brandon stopped, biting his tongue. The shadow of a man fell across the floor. Piet Lientzget bulked in the doorway.

'So that's where you're all hiding!' he said with a leer. 'I was looking for you.'

Vetjek pulled himself together. 'Oh yes; you had some news for me, Piet. What is it? You can speak freely in front of Brandon. He's one of us.'

Lientzget sniffed rudely. 'Is he?' His tone was suspicious. 'Very well, then. I just thought you'd like to know I've been to the northeast today with some of the instruments. There's no gold there, Hans, but it looks pretty rich in sulphur.' He grinned vindictively at Ingrid. 'Forestalled you, didn't I?' he sneered. 'And you a sulphur expert — I don't think!' He turned on his heel, making to leave. Brandon stopped him.

'Have you told anyone else?' he demanded.

Lientzget eyed him insolently. 'Sure,' he replied. 'They all know. Why not? Sulphur's all right, but it's gold we're after.'

'Oh my God!' muttered Vetjek. His face was almost comic in its helplessness.

Brandon took a deep, slow, painful breath, aware that Lientzget was watching him curiously. He met the man's gaze. 'All right,' he said. 'That lets you out, at any rate.'

Lientzget frowned. 'I think you're all a

little mad,' he said. Then he thumped out of the room with a disdainful grunt.

They looked at one another. 'So it's common knowledge,' murmured Brandon bitterly. 'You know what that means . . . ? Annihilation tonight if we don't find our man!' Neither Vetjek nor Ingrid had any answer.

Brandon went out through the door. He paused on the darkening snow, staring at the rising hump of Ectal Borrn where it climbed like a stranded whale against the grey of oncoming night. A mountain of gold. But the gold was sulphur — more deadly to their lives than poison at the moment.

The main door of the cabin opened and Tony Bayne appeared with Weston. Their faces were flushed and excited. 'You've heard Piet's news?' burst out Bayne. 'Sulphur, Hans! Isn't that just what the doctor ordered?'

'We'll verify it first thing tomorrow,' added Weston. He rubbed his hands together and grinned at Ingrid.

Grants came from round the corner of the cabin. He, too, had heard the news.

Which man? Brandon's thoughts were desperate. *Which man?*

Grants, in the middle of a sentence, broke off and listened, head to one side, face screwed up. Brandon heard it, too. The growing drone of an aircraft. They crowded in the open door, everyone in the camp except Nicolas Shawn, staring upwards at the rapidly darkening sky. Stephanie was the first to pick out the plane. It showed black against the sky, and it circled the camp. A moment later, a signal light floated down from the fuselage, and the plane began to drop more steeply.

'He's landing!' gasped Tony Bayne in surprise.

Brandon watched the aircraft land and taxi across the snow towards them. 'Well, I'll be damned!' he muttered half to himself.

'What's the matter?' asked Stephanie. She was close to Sergeant Brown, her arm through his.

'It's Henri's ship!' answered Brandon.

The plane came to rest. A figure appeared at the cabin door and dropped to the ground, to be followed by a second, floundering in the snow.

'Your pardon,' said Henri politely, 'but we land 'ere to tell you *M'sieu* Brandon disappear. I was to bring 'im, but we 'ave ze crash. Then we lose 'im. 'E was a fine man; so brave. Never do I see — '

Brandon stepped forward, smiling. The pilot gave a whoop of joy, running to embrace him, much to everyone's amusement.

As they all filed indoors, it was Archibald Ramshorn who trailed along in the rear, muttering to himself. Then came further confused introductions. Henri said he would park his plane under some trees for the night; in the morning he must take Ramshorn on to his destination.

Ramshorn stood with his back to the stove, looking at his hosts, while Henri was outside parking the plane. 'Jeez!' he said wearily. 'This is some country, ain't it? Can I sell you people any sanitary perquisites? If you have a bathroom or a closet, now . . . ?' He looked round hopefully.

Tony Bayne chuckled. 'You'd better ask Weston that,' he said. 'He's our sanitary expert on this location.'

Weston looked up from the magazine he was reading. 'Sorry,' he said, 'but we're all fixed up, thank you. No sale, I'm afraid.'

'You won't get much out of Hiram,' put in Grants with a grin. 'He's inclined to be close with the dough!'

Ramshorn blinked and glanced at Weston. 'You one of these geologist fellers?' he enquired.

Weston nodded pleasantly.

'Hiram Weston . . . ' mused Ramshorn slowly. 'Mister, you sure have changed since I sold you that disinfectant a few months back.'

Brandon felt prickles running up and down his neck. His eyes were fixed on Weston. The others looked on amusedly.

Weston put his magazine down. 'You must be mixing me up with someone else,' he said quietly.

But the little bag-man shook his head. 'No, sir!' he said with conviction. 'I ain't so bad at faces, bud.'

Weston rose from his chair, all eyes on him now. He gave a shrug and made for the door of the cabin. Outside, the roar of Henri's engine was fluctuating as he taxied the plane.

Brandon moved. 'Stop that man!' he shouted curtly.

Weston shot him one look and dived for the door, dragging a gun from his pocket as he went. The crash of a shot echoed in the night. Then Weston was racing for the trees.

The others poured out in his wake. Even Nick Shawn, his face still bandaged, was there in the rear; and the two women as well. Only Archibald Ramshorn stood shaking his head in the doorway of the cabin. 'Aw, nuts,' he said succinctly, going back to the stove.

The gun bellowed again and a bullet sung past Brandon's head. Then Weston saw the plane, still moving over the snow. He altered course and ran towards it desperately. Henri saw him coming and stopped the aircraft, jumping to the ground in his curiosity to see what was happening. Weston reached him, felled him with a blow from the automatic he carried, and leapt into the cabin, slamming the door.

Brandon came to a panting halt, the rest crowding up around him. The plane was driving full bore across the flattened snow.

'Lost him!' said Vetjek bitterly.

Henri groaned and sat up, rubbing his head. '*Mon Dieu!*' he muttered. 'My plane!'

They watched in silence. The plane bounced, almost lost to sight in the darkness. Then it seemed to stop abruptly, the engine note changed, and the tail reared up. A great gout of flame enveloped the fuselage. Henri covered his face with his hands.

'He's hit a crevice,' said Bayne in an awed whisper. 'Poor devil. I could have told him there was one over there.'

They started running, but before they were halfway to the burning aircraft Brandon knew it was hopeless. The heat drove them off. For one second a blackened figure moved in the inferno of the cabin, then fell back out of sight, to be swallowed in the greedy flames.

They returned to the camp in silence. Ramshorn looked up as Brandon entered. 'You know what?' he said suddenly. 'Maybe I was mixing that feller up with someone else. Weston ain't such an uncommon name.'

Brandon shook his head. 'You didn't make a mistake,' he said.

Vetjek patted the surprised little bagman on the shoulder. 'We'll place an order with you, my friend,' he said. 'A big one, you understand?'

Ramshorn blinked. 'You mean you've got a toilet in this dump?' he said incredulously. 'Gee, ain't that wonderful!'

'There's something else here, too,' said Brandon curtly. 'Grants, have you lost any blasting material since arriving?'

Grants frowned. 'I'll check,' he said, and was gone. When he came back, there was a puzzled look on his face. 'What do you think?' he blurted out. 'There's something like a half-ton of ammonite missing from the store. Enough to wreck a town!'

'Enough to wipe out everyone here,

you mean,' said Brandon. 'If you're wise, you'll tear this floor up and find it — now!'

They did.

Talk went on far into the night. Shawn used the radio and made a report, obtaining permission to stay on at Great Bear as part of the expedition. Stephanie, too, used the radio. Everyone was cheerful — except perhaps Stephanie, at the prospect of losing Sergeant Brown for a time. Even Piet Lientzget joked and made friends.

'And tomorrow,' said Vetjek, 'we'll start our real work.'

'Sulphur!' whispered Ingrid, sipping a mug of coffee, her eyes warm and shining as she looked across at Shawn.

But probably the happiest person present was Ramshorn. *He* had obtained an order in a territory with a hitherto negative sales record. It was a big day in Ramshorn's life.

We do hope that you have enjoyed reading this large print book.

Did you know that all of our titles are available for purchase?

We publish a wide range of high quality large print books including:
Romances, Mysteries, Classics
General Fiction
Non Fiction and Westerns

Special interest titles available in large print are:
The Little Oxford Dictionary
Music Book, Song Book
Hymn Book, Service Book

Also available from us courtesy of Oxford University Press:
Young Readers' Dictionary
(large print edition)
Young Readers' Thesaurus
(large print edition)

For further information or a free brochure, please contact us at:
Ulverscroft Large Print Books Ltd.,
The Green, Bradgate Road, Anstey,
Leicester, LE7 7FU, England.
Tel: (00 44) **0116 236 4325**
Fax: (00 44) **0116 234 0205**

BACKGROUND FOR MURDER

Shelley Smith

In a psychiatric hospital, the head doctor lies dead — his skull smashed in with a brass poker. Private investigator Jacob Chaos is called in by Scotland Yard to investigate. But there are many people who might have wished harm upon Dr. Royd: the patients who resented his cruel treatment methods; the doctors who harboured jealousy of his position; even his own wife. With Dr. Helen Crawford as the Watson to his Holmes, Chaos must untangle the threads of the mystery . . .

THE LIBRARY DETECTIVE RETURNS

James Holding

Former Homicide cop Hal Johnson now works as 'library fuzz' — spending his days chasing down overdue books, stolen volumes, and owed fines. He doesn't miss life in the fast lane. But his police training and detective instincts still prove necessary in the bibliographic delinquency division. For such apparently innocuous peccadillos on the part of borrowers often set Hal on the trail towards uncovering greater crimes: fraud, theft, drug-smuggling, arson — and even murder . . .

DEAD MAN'S PAIN

Valerie Holmes

A man being pursued collides with
Nicholas Penn. Assuming his pocket
has been pilfered in the scuffle,
Nicholas also gives chase. But the
stranger fails to see a horse careering
down the road, and is trampled by the
animal, seemingly mortally. Later,
though, Nicholas discovers that the
man was no thief — and still lives.
Mystified, he is determined to discover the truth behind the 'dead'
man's pain . . .

MORE SECRET FILES OF SHERLOCK HOLMES

Gary Lovisi

Five untold tales of the great detective. In the first, Holmes chronicles to Watson a strange event at a freak show years before he met the good doctor. The second sees Watson throwing a birthday party for his friend — but danger lurks among the festivities. The detective and the doctor play golf at St. Andrews, and then are invited to Paris to solve a most perplexing art theft. Finally, Conan Doyle's Professor Challenger meets the duo, who arrive in the hope of preventing an attempt on his life.

THE HUNTSMAN

Gerald Verner

Superintendent Budd is faced with one of his toughest assignments in separating the strands of mystery that grip the village of Chalebury: a series of robberies perpetrated by the burglar known as Stocking-foot; sightings of the ghostly Huntsman; and the murders of a villager and a local police inspector. Interweaving with these is the suspicious behaviour of a frightened young woman who lives in a large dilapidated house with one elderly servant. Is there a connection between all these crimes and other oddities happening in the tiny village?

DREAMS IN THE NIGHT

Norman Firth

Tiring of her repressed life on a country farm, teenage beauty Alice Graham runs away from home, hoping to find a job as a journalist in New York in the Roaring Twenties. When her money runs out and she is on the edge of despair, she is befriended by Maddie, a veteran of the burlesque theatre, who takes her under her wing. But Alice soon attracts the unwelcome attentions of a New York gangster, which begins a chain of events that ignites a powder keg of murder and ultimate tragedy . . .